THE
Promise

SHANELL KEYS

Copyright © 2023 Shanell Keys.

All rights reserved. No part of this book may be reproduced, stored, or transmitted by any means—whether auditory, graphic, mechanical, or electronic—without written permission of both publisher and author, except in the case of brief excerpts used in critical articles and reviews. Unauthorized reproduction of any part of this work is illegal and is punishable by law.

ISBN: 979-8-88640-663-4 (sc)
ISBN: 979-8-88640-664-1 (hc)
ISBN: 979-8-88640-665-8 (e)

Because of the dynamic nature of the Internet, any web addresses or links contained in this book may have changed since publication and may no longer be valid. The views expressed in this work are solely those of the author and do not necessarily reflect the views of the publisher, and the publisher hereby disclaims any responsibility for them.

One Galleria Blvd., Suite 1900, Metairie, LA 70001
1-888-421-2397

CHAPTER

I've always felt like I was invisible. Most people feel that way every once in a while, but I've felt that way every single day. I walk around doing the same things everyone else does, but nobody notices me, not really. Sure, people stop to ask for directions, take my order in the fast-food line, and even make small talk at the bus station. But nobody takes the time to get to know me on a deeper level. Nobody cares enough to figure out what makes Rachel Walters tick. Nobody, that is, until I met Sam. He saw something in me that nobody else did, and he loved me for the imperfect person I am. For me, that will always be more than enough. I met Sam for the first time in second-period world history, and let's just say he didn't make a great first impression. He strolled in ten minutes late for class while the teacher, Mrs. Nichols, was writing something on the whiteboard. I attended the Bright Academy, a ritzy private high school in Sacramento. While most of my classmates had rich parents to pay the very high tuition, I didn't. I was there on a full scholarship because of my good grades. This scholarship was only awarded to ten students in the whole country and could be taken away at any time if I messed up. That's why people like Sam Goodwin got on my last nerve. I was one of the rare students who was actually there to learn. Sam slipped into the seat behind mine and let out a sigh of relief.

"I hope you have a good reason for being late, Mr. Goodwin," Mrs. Nichols said sternly. She always wore her jet-black hair in a super tight bun, and she almost never smiled. She probably had the sense of humor of a lump of coal.

Sam looked like a deer caught in the headlights, and I had to laugh a little.

Sam paused for a minute, probably trying to think of some lame excuse to get out of detention. Then, a big, dopey grin spread over his face. "Of course, I do. My toaster caught on fire."

"Your toaster caught on fire?" Mrs. Nichols repeated. Sam nodded sadly. "Yes, it did. And we didn't have any cereal, so I had to cook myself some eggs. I could have come on an empty stomach, but I probably wouldn't be learning much anyway. Plus, the growling sound would be very disruptive to the class. So really, I was just doing everyone a favor."

The class erupted in laughter, but the teacher didn't look amused. "Well, since it's the first week of school, I won't give you detention—this time. But I won't be so lenient in the future. Now, I would like everyone to turn to page 20 in your textbooks."

I started flipping through my textbook when I felt a tap on my shoulder. It was Sam, and of course, he didn't have his book.

"Can I look on with you?" he asked.

I sighed and held the book between us.

At lunch that day, I sat in the back of the cafeteria, eating my sandwich and taking notes out of my English book at the same time. In high school, it's important for most people to belong to a group. There was Jessica Sinclair and the popular group and Ryan Slater and his group of skaters. There was even a group for all of the nerds. It was called chess club. I was not like most people, and I was perfectly happy eating my sandwich all by myself. Between my schoolwork and my job at Burger Shack, I didn't really have time for friends anyway. So I wasn't at all pleased when Sam plopped himself down next to me with that big, dopey grin on his face.

"Do you mind if I sit here?" he asked, as if he weren't already sitting.

"It's a free country."

"I'm Sam. Sam Goodwin."

"Rachel Walters," I said without looking up from my book.

"What are you reading?"

"My English book. We have a quiz coming up, so I really need to study."

He took a bite of his sandwich, staring at me like he was trying to read what I was thinking. It kind of gave me the creeps. Then he asked, "Is there a reason you don't like me?"

"I never said I don't like you."

"Well, you do give off this vibe like you want me to disappear."

"I guess it's not working then," I said sarcastically.

He laughed. "Well, I'd like to make a bet with you. I bet by the end of the school year, you won't be able to get enough of me."

"You're on, but I have to warn you. I'm one tough nut to crack. You might have more luck with someone like Jessica

Sinclair." I gestured toward her, and Jessica smiled a flirtatious grin and tucked a strand of her long blonde hair behind her ear. "See. I think she likes you."

Sam shook his head. "There's a problem with that."

"What's the problem? She's the lead cheerleader, and she's drop-dead gorgeous—every man's dream."

"Not mine."

"Why not?"

"Because I'm not interested in Jessica. I'm interested in you."

I felt a lump form in my throat all of a sudden, and it was hard to breathe. I had no idea how to respond to that. Luckily, I was saved by the sound of the bell.

"We should get to class," I said, scooping up the remainders of my lunch.

"Let me walk with you," Sam said. "I have to go that way for Spanish class anyway."

I swallowed the lump in my throat. "Okay." That's when I knew I was in trouble, and he just might win that bet after all.

CHAPTER

2

People always say I give off a vibe that makes them want to stay away. If I do, it's only a defense mechanism. If I never let people get too close, there's no chance they can hurt me. Besides, if they knew how crappy my life really is, they would want to stay as far away from me as possible. So, I'm really just saving them time.

After school that day, I let myself into my apartment like I always did. I threw my keys down on top of the stack of unpaid bills. My kid sister, Michelle, was sprawled out on the couch watching *General Hospital*. A bowl of cheeseballs sat in front of her, and her fingers were painted bright orange. Her long dark hair was a tangled mess, which reminded me it was time to take her in for a haircut soon. I wondered when I would find time for that. She looked up at me and smiled.

"Hi, Rachel."

"Hey, squirt. How was your day?" I asked.

She shrugged. "All right, I guess."

"Did you do your homework?"

She rolled her eyes. "I hate homework. Besides, the math is way too hard. It looks like Chinese."

"Remember what we talked about?" I asked, sounding more like her mother than her big sister. In many ways, I guess I was.

"Yes. Sometimes we have to do things we don't want to do," she said with a sigh.

"That's right. Now, I want you to circle the problems you're having trouble with, and I'll help you after dinner."

She walked toward our room, mumbling to herself.

"How's Mom today?" I asked.

"The same as she was yesterday and the day before that," she told me before she closed the door behind her.

I walked into Mom's room, where she lay in her bed, doped up on pain killers. She'd slipped into a deep depression after Dad died, which was almost ten years ago. She spent about 80 percent of the time in a drug-induced sleep, but even when she was awake, it was like she wasn't even there. She'd had more jobs than I could count, and she'd *lost* every single one of them. I'd gotten pretty good at making excuses for her. *She's not feeling well today. Her grandmother died. She has a doctor's appointment.* Her bosses were as understanding as they could be, but it was only a matter of time before they figured out the excuses were obviously not true. How many grandmothers can one person have, anyway? Sometimes I felt sorry for her, but most of the time I was just angry because she seemed to forget about the people who were alive.

That night I cooked a frozen pizza for dinner. Not that there were a lot of options. Our fridge was pretty much empty, which meant we would be eating a lot of Top Ramen until my next pay day. At least Burger Shack let me bring home some of the extra food from wrong orders or orders that nobody picked up. You would be surprised how often that happened.

Mom came out just long enough to eat. I noticed she was wearing the same tattered T-shirt and jeans she'd been wearing all week. She was starting to smell too. Not that she cared enough to take a shower.

"I got the lead in the school play," Michelle announced proudly. "It's called *A Fairy Tale*, and I get to play Princess Rianna."

"That's great," I said. "You'll be perfect for that part. I wrote that play when I was in middle school, you know. Is Mr. Corban still the drama teacher?"

Michelle nodded. "Yes, and he's really nice. He said it was the perfect part for me. I nailed the audition."

"It's not going to cost anything, is it?" Mom asked as she picked a piece of pepperoni off of her pizza.

Michelle shook her head. "Nope. They're using the same costumes they did last year."

"Why does it matter to you anyway, Mother?" I interrupted. "It's not like you'd be the one paying for it."

She didn't have a comeback—probably because she knew I was right. We all ate the rest of our dinner in silence.

That night after we all took our showers, I brushed Michelle's hair one hundred strokes. She could brush her own hair, but I think she liked the attention, and I didn't mind doing it. After we turned the lights out, we lay there for a long time, not saying anything, until Michelle broke the silence.

"Rachel, do you think Mom will ever be normal again?"

I laughed. "What's normal?"

"You know what I mean."

I sighed. "I don't know, kiddo."

"What was she like before?"

I thought for a minute. It was getting harder and harder to remember. "Well, I guess she was just a normal mom. She was happy, and she smiled all the time. She had a deep belly laugh—just like you."

Michelle giggled. "It's hard to imagine Mom laughing like that."

"Well, she did. A long, long time ago."

"Tell me about Dad."

"I've told you about him."

"Tell me again."

"Well, he was one of the kindest people you could ever meet. He always smelled like coffee, and he loved music. He played in a band, so our house was always full of people. It was a lot of fun. Most of all, he loved us. He used to toss us up in the air and catch us all the time. He was just like a big kid … full of life." *Until he wasn't.*

My sister and I lay there for the longest time, basking in our fantasy life—the one we both wish we still had.

"Rachel?"

"Yeah, squirt?"

"Promise me something?"

"What?"

"Promise you'll never leave me. I couldn't take it on my own."

"I promise," I mumbled as I drifted off to sleep.

CHAPTER

3

"Mom should be here to pick you up after school," I told Michelle as I pulled up in front of her middle school the next morning.

Michelle rolled her eyes. "I'll believe that when I see it. I'm used to walking home, anyway."

I always felt a little guilty on the days I had to work because I knew nobody would be there for Michelle. She was nearly thirteen, but she still needed someone to make sure she did her homework and had dinner. In a normal family, that person would be the parent. But we didn't have a normal family. We were the poster family for dysfunctional.

"Maybe I can pick you up and bring you with me to work," I said. "I'll bring you some food, and you can do your homework."

She shook her head. "That's all right. You already got in trouble for doing that, remember? Besides, I have rehearsal for the play after school."

"Okay, call me at Burger Shack if you need anything."

"I will."

"See you later, squirt. And good luck with the rehearsal. I know you'll rock this part."

"Thanks. See you!"

I watched as she walked into the schoolyard before I headed off for my own school.

⁂

It seemed like a quiet day at the Bright Academy until Sam ran up to me, proudly waving his book in the air.

"I brought my book today," he said, as if it weren't obvious.

I continued walking toward my class. "I hope you put it to good use."

He started walking faster, practically jogging to keep up with me. "I wanted to ask you something. There is a new ice cream parlor opening down the street. I heard they have some flavors you can't get anywhere else. I wondered if you might like to go with me after school."

"I can't. I have to work."

"Oh. Where do you work?"

"Burger Shack."

"Cool. I heard they have the best fries in town."

"They're okay. Listen, Sam. You seem like a really nice guy, which is why I want to make this crystal clear before you get your feelings hurt. I am not looking for any sort of relationship right now. My life is just way too ... complicated."

"I'll wait until it's less complicated then."

"You'll probably be waiting a long time."

"You're worth the wait."

Burger Shack was crazy busy like it always was on free fryday. Everyone got a free order of fries when they ordered one of our famous burgers, so it was one of our busiest days. And, of course, three of my coworkers had called in sick, leaving me with about a hundred costumers all by myself. I didn't mind when it was busy because I didn't have time to think about certain things I didn't want to think about— things like the bills that needed to be paid; my strung-out, depressed, drug-addict mom; my sister who needed me to be less of a sister and more of a mom; and Sam. So, I wasn't exactly jumping for joy when I saw him sitting at a table in the back of Burger Shack, casually thumbing through a menu. I thought to myself that this guy must be mental. I mean, didn't he have anything better to do? Was he stalking me? I was going to put an end to this right now. I marched over to his table on a mission.

"What are you doing here?" I demanded.

He shrugged. "I'm just here to get something to eat." I sighed and pulled my notepad out of my apron. "What do you want?"

"I'll have the chili cheese fries and a chocolate milkshake."

I rolled my eyes. "You do know that has enough calories to kill an elephant, right?"

"I don't care. I like to live on the edge."

"Suit yourself." I took his menu and headed back to the kitchen.

I continued doing my job, refilling drinks and bringing people their orders. Sam was staring at me the whole time with a ridiculous grin on his face. I tried my best to ignore him, but it wasn't easy. Something about his eyes made my stomach do flip-flops. That just made me mad because I knew that I couldn't have feelings for him, and even if I did, I couldn't let him know it. It would never work between us for more reasons than I could count.

When his order was finally ready, I plopped it on his table. "Here's your heart attack."

He shoved a handful of fries in his mouth and washed them down with a swig of the chocolate shake. Then he sat back, savoring it. "This is so good! Do you want some?"

"No thanks," I said even though I hadn't eaten much all day, and the smell of the food was making my stomach growl. "You know, there are at least ten burger joints within a mile from here. So why did you have to come to this one?" He shrugged. "They don't have chili cheese fries, and they don't have you."

CHAPTER

4

From that day forward, I had a shadow, and his name was Sam Goodwin. Wherever I was, he was sure to be about two steps behind me. He still annoyed me sometimes, but I had to admit that the company was nice. If anything, he added humor to my lame excuse for a life. The best part was he didn't ask about my homelife. There were just some things I didn't want him to know.

After school one day, I found him waiting by my car. "Hey, Rachel. I was wondering if you could do me a favor."

"Depends on what it is," I said as I unlocked the driver's side door.

"Could you give me a ride home? My dad was supposed to pick me up, but he got stuck in a meeting."

I looked at my watch. "I guess so, as long as it's not too far. I have work today."

Before I even finished my sentence, he'd already slipped into the passenger seat. "Thanks," he said.

It was mostly a quiet drive, except for Sam's occasional directions.

"Turn right at the signal."

I began to realize he was leading me to a very rich neighborhood. Most of the houses looked like mansions, and it made me feel a little nervous for some strange reason— like I was out of my element and didn't belong.

"It's the third house on the right," he told me.

My jaw dropped when I looked up at the humungous house. In the center of the driveway was a fountain, and there were tennis courts to the left. I could see a swimming pool in the back, and everything was accented with a perfectly manicured lawn that looked too beautiful to walk on and landscaping that belonged in a home and garden show.

"Do you want to come in for a Coke or something?" Sam asked, bringing me back to reality.

I hesitated. I had a little time before my shift at Burger Shack, but I didn't want him to know that.

"Come on, you don't have to stay long. I'd feel better if I could repay you for the ride home."

"All right. For a little bit, I guess."

"This is the living room," Sam said as he led me through a room that was bigger than my entire apartment. Two white couches sat in the center, along with antique end tables. The artwork that decorated the walls looked like it was worth a fortune. "And right through here is the entertainment room where we watch movies and play video games."

I took a sip of my cherry Coke and gulped nervously. "This is quite some place."

Sam looked at me like he was trying to read what I was thinking. "Is everything okay?"

I nodded. "Yes. It's just ... You didn't tell me your parents are—"

"Rich?" He finished the sentence for me. "It's not really something I like to brag about, honestly. My dad is the president of Goodwin Financial. He's very successful, but he's at work all the time. He never came to any of my soccer games or school events. If I had a choice, I would trade all of this for a dad who was present."

I stood there in silence for a minute, trying to take it all in. I thought to myself that I would give anything for a dad who was *alive*. Sam Goodwin didn't know how lucky he was. Just then, a woman bounced into the room. She had super straight blonde hair that obviously came out of a bottle, and she was dressed like she was in her twenties, even though she looked like she was in her mid-forties. Her huge pouty lips screamed Botox, and her cheeks and eyes looked like they might have had some work too.

"Sam, you're home!" she squealed. "I was going to send Geoffrey to come pick you up."

Then she looked at me—more like she was inspecting me. "Who's your little friend?"

Sam cleared his throat. "Mom, this is Rachel. Rachel, this is my mom, Norma."

"Hi," I said quietly, looking down at my tattered sneakers and feeling the overwhelming urge to get out of there as quickly as possible. "I really should get going, I don't want to be late for work."

CHAPTER

"Rachel, wait up!" Sam called as he ran to catch up with me the next morning.

"What?" I asked, impatiently. I slowed down just long enough for him to catch up.

"I just wanted to apologize if my mom made you uncomfortable yesterday. She tends to do that sometimes."

"She didn't." I lied.

"Are you sure? Because you left in a hurry. I just hope she didn't chase you away."

"I had to get to work," I said flatly. "I can't afford to be late."

He nodded. "I know. Thanks again for giving me a ride home. You didn't have to do that. I have a little confession to make: I could have had our driver pick me up, but I wanted an excuse to spend some time with you."

I sighed. "You really aren't going to give it up, are you?" He looked at me, confused. "Give what up?"

"This idea that we are going to be more than friends. I already told you that isn't going to happen. Not now and probably not ever." My heart was pounding in my chest, like it always seemed to do when Sam was around. But I knew I had to ignore my pounding heart and the butterflies in my stomach. Sam and I were from two completely different worlds. He was way out of my league. "You're a really nice guy, and I like you ... I really do. But I need you to stop following me around and looking at me like I'm a piece of candy."

He snorted. "I do not look at you like you're a piece of candy. But if you were a piece of candy, you would probably be chocolate. Not just any ordinary chocolate, but the kind they sell at that fancy store in the mall that's shipped in from Switzerland. The one that sits in the display window with lights around it because it's so awesome."

I shook my head. "This needs to stop right now, Sam. I want to be your friend, I really do. But if you can't respect some boundaries, then I don't know if I can."

I turned around and marched off to class without looking back.

That day, I took Michelle in for a long-overdue haircut.

Our hairdresser, Vanna, looked up at us and smiled.

"Long time no see."

"I know. It's been a while." I said. "Michelle is definitely due for a haircut."

"Well, she will look like a model when I'm done with her," Vanna said with a wink.

Vanna worked her magic on Michelle's hair, cutting it into long layers that fell to her shoulders in wispy cascades. Her frizzy, unmanageable hair now had a sleek shine to it, and she smiled when she looked at her reflection in the mirror. I handed Vanna some money before we headed home.

⁂

"Mom, we're home!" Michelle called as she danced into the house. "Look at my new haircut!" She did a little twirl, clearly proud of her new do.

Mom sat on the couch in the living room with a faraway look on her face, trembling. She looked up and shook her head. "Is that where you two have been all afternoon? I was worried sick. And did you even think about the fact that you have the only running car? I needed to get my medication, but I had no way to get there. Did you even think about that? Do you ever think of anyone besides yourself, or are you really that selfish?"

I took a deep breath. I knew very well that *medication* was just her code word for drugs. "I always think about you, Mom. I told you I'm trying to save up enough money to fix Dad's old car, but with all the other bills, it's just hard. There's never enough. And Michelle really needed a haircut. Maybe if you would just get your head out of your ass for a change, you would have noticed that."

"Shut up, Rachel!" she snapped. "No daughter of mine is going to talk to me that way. This is going to end right now!" She stood up and grabbed a pair of scissors off the table. Then she marched toward Michelle on a mission. She grabbed Michelle by the neck and started hacking away at her hair. Michelle tried to fight her off, but she was bigger and stronger.

"No, Mom! Stop!" I screamed. "Leave her alone!" I struggled to pry the scissors out of her hand, but it was no use. The damage had already been done. Michelle's beautiful brown hair was a bunch of uneven tuffs.

When Mom was finally finished demolishing Michelle's hair, she stood up, looking proud of herself. Then she grabbed the keys from the table and marched out the door. I heard the engine start and the tires on the pavement as she backed out of the driveway. Michelle burst into tears.

"I look like a freak!" she sobbed as she ran into our room and slammed the door behind her.

After I had given my sister some time to calm down, I softly knocked on the door.

"Leave me alone!" she snapped.

I walked in anyway. My heart sank when I saw her sitting on her bed crying. I sat down beside her and put my arm around her.

"I was so excited to show my friends my new haircut," she said through her tears. "Now it just looks awful."

I ran my fingers through the uneven tufts of hair that remained. "I think I can fix this."

She looked up at me with hope in her big brown eyes. "Really?"

I nodded. "I gave myself a haircut once. This can't be too different, can it?"

I grabbed a pair of scissors from my nightstand drawer and went to work. When I was done, it didn't look half bad for an amateur cut.

"Thanks, Rachel."

"You're welcome, kiddo. I'm really sorry about what Mom did."

"It's not your fault," she said. "But we really need to get her some help—like rehab. I can't live like this anymore. All she thinks about is how to get her next fix."

"I know, but she has to want help." I reminded her. "Mom doesn't want help. She just wants to blame everyone else."

"Maybe we should stage an intervention, then," Michelle added.

"We tried that last year, remember? It lasted about a day. She promised to get help, but she never did."

She nodded. "Yeah, I remember. But maybe this time could be different. It doesn't hurt to dream, does it?"

I tussled her hair. "No, kiddo. It doesn't hurt to dream."

CHAPTER

6

When Michelle and I came home from school the next day, the apartment was cleaner than it had been in months, and it smelled like something was cooking.

Mom stood over the stove, stirring something in a pot. "Hi, girls. How was your day? I hope you're hungry. I'm making pot roast for dinner."

I rolled my eyes. Whenever Mom blew up like she had the day before, she felt the need to make it up to us the next day. Sometimes it was in the form of food, or sometimes we would do something fun together. She seemed to forget about all of the hurtful things she had said and morphed into this bubbly supermom. I never knew how long her high would last, and I always felt like I was just waiting for the bottom to drop out again. So, I didn't get excited when she was in a good mood anymore. I knew it was as phony as a three-dollar bill. I also knew it was short-lived. As soon as her drugs wore off again, she would change back into the self-centered person I hated. It was a vicious cycle.

She gave Michelle a kiss on the cheek. "Your hair looks great!"

Michelle just groaned and ran off to our room. Mom looked at me, confused. "What's her problem?"

I shrugged. "I don't know. Listen, Mom. I wanted you to know I'm working the late shift at Burger Shack tomorrow."

"No problem. You know you can have the car as long as you need it. And I hope you know I appreciate everything you do for us, Rachel. I'm very proud of you."

"Thanks, Mom."

"I love you."

"Love you too." I said, almost believing it.

After everyone was in bed that night, I sat in the living room, watching some old home videos. I didn't watch them very often because they always seemed to upset Mom. But every once in a while, I got sentimental and needed to see us the way we were before.

We were on a family vacation in Santa Cruz just a few months before Dad died. We all looked so happy, running around on the beach. Michelle and I were so young. I was seven, and she was only two. Dad and I were trying to build a sand castle, while Michelle tried to knock it down. Then he scooped us both up in his arms, and we looked up and waved at the camera with big smiles on our faces. Mom must have been the one filming, but it was probably the last time she made a home movie. There aren't very many pictures or videos taken after Dad died. I was mesmerized by the light of the TV, in my own world. So I was startled when I heard someone come up behind me.

"What are you watching?"

I looked up and saw Mom standing over me. Her expression was somewhere between shock and anger, and her eyes seemed cold.

"Oh, nothing," I said, quickly hitting the stop button on the remote.

She sat down beside me. "You know, Rachel, those movies aren't going to bring him back."

"I know."

"He's gone forever."

I glared at her. "You think I don't know that?!" I could feel the tears trailing down my cheek. "Sometimes I'm afraid I'll forget him."

"Well, maybe we would all be better off if we did forget." I felt my bottom lip tremble. "You don't mean that."

"Yes, I do. I think all of these memories make us all sad. Look at you right now. You're crying."

"Maybe that's not such a bad thing," I said through my tears.

"I don't think it does anybody any good," she said sharply. "As a matter of fact, I think it's time to put an end to it."

She stood up and pushed the eject button on the DVD player.

"What are you doing, Mom?" I asked, my voice cracking. She didn't answer. She just threw the DVD on the floor and started stomping on it.

"Stop it!" I screamed, pushing her out of the way.

She fell backward onto the couch, but the DVD was already smashed into several jagged pieces.

My tears came faster now, and I bent down, holding the broken pieces together, as if I could magically fix it. "Why did you do that?" I demanded.

Now she was bawling like a baby. "I don't know," she said in a high-pitched voice. "I'm so sorry, for everything." I wrapped my arms around her, and we cried and held each other for what seemed like hours. As much as I wanted to hate her, I knew she was just hurting—like I was. I just wondered when the hurt would finally end.

CHAPTER

7

Work was slow the next day, and I couldn't wait for my shift to end. I was just getting ready to lock up when a shiny red Camaro pulled into the parking lot. I quickly flipped the sign around in the window to the side that said closed, but Sam hopped out of the car and walked up to the door anyway.

"Of course," I mumbled to myself, realizing that this guy really wasn't going to give up. He was something else— and not in a good way. "We're closed."

"I know," he said. "I just want to talk to you for a minute."

I unlocked the door and opened it. "Did you hear anything I said the other day?"

He nodded. "Yes, I did."

"Is this what you call respecting boundaries? Following me around school and to work?"

"I know I really shouldn't be here, but I need some help with something. I tried to talk to you at school, but you just ignored me, so I figured this was the best place to talk to you."

"How did you know I'd be working this late?" I asked, suspicious.

Sam shrugged. "Just a hunch."

"Okay, so what did you want to talk about?"

"Well, here's the thing. I'm really not doing so great at school."

I snorted. "That doesn't surprise me. I mean, you're late all the time, and you hardly pay any attention to what the teacher is saying."

"I'm not late. The bell just rings way too early," he said with that dopey grin on his face. "And I can't pay attention because I'm too busy looking at you."

My pulse started to quicken at the sound of his words. I cleared my throat. "So, what do your poor grades have to do with me?"

"Well, if I don't get my grades up, I will get kicked off the basketball team, and my parents will kill me. So, I could really use a tutor. I know you're really smart, so I was hoping you could do it. In return, I will pay you every week. Double what you make here at Burger Shack."

I gulped. "That's a lot of money for tutoring. I would do it for a lot less, but I don't want your charity. I don't like people doing things for me because they feel sorry for me." He shook his head. "I don't feel sorry for you, Rachel. The exact opposite. You're the smartest person I know, so I just wanted to offer you the job first."

An awkward silence filled the air while I thought. The extra money could change everything for us. We wouldn't have to eat Top Ramen and Burger Shack rejects all the time anymore. Maybe I could finally fix Dad's old car so we could drive it again.

THE PROMISE

I could catch up on the bills, so the collectors would stop calling. And maybe I could finally afford a haircut for myself.

"Okay, I'll do it."

Sam's grin grew even bigger. "That's good news. Thanks."

I nodded. "Don't get any ideas, though. This is strictly professional."

He straightened up a bit. "Of course."

I looked out the window at the shiny red Camaro that was parked next to my beat-up old Volkswagen. "Nice car."

"Thanks. I just got it today. It was a birthday present from my parents."

"Today is your birthday?"

He nodded. "Yep, eighteen today. It's no big deal, really. After my parents gave me the car, they jumped on a plane to Paris."

I could feel my eyes widen. "You mean you didn't even get a birthday cake for your eighteenth birthday? No party or anything?"

"I guess my parents thought Paris was more important," he said with a shrug. "Anyway, I guess I should get going. It's getting late, and I know you were trying to lock up. We can talk about the tutoring schedule tomorrow, okay?"

All of a sudden, I felt sorry for him. He deserved some sort of celebration for his birthday, especially his eighteenth. It didn't seem right that his parents would ignore his birthday like that. Well, I guess technically they didn't ignore it. They gave him a car. But I still wanted to do something more for him.

"Wait here for a minute," I said. "I'll be right back."

I ran back to the kitchen and grabbed a huge slice of our famous triple chocolate cake. It was the best chocolate cake known to man, and people sometimes came to Burger Shack just for the cake. It was really that good. I quickly decorated it with some colorful sprinkles we had stashed away for special occasions and finished it off with a candle. Sam was beaming when I came back out with the cake.

"Happy birthday, Sam," I said.

"Thanks. You didn't have to do that."

"I know I didn't *have* to. I wanted to. Now hurry up and blow out the candle. It's melting. And don't forget to make a wish."

He took a deep breath in and blew out the candle. Small puffs of smoke and the smell of melting wax lingered in the air.

"Hey, I've got an idea," he said. "Why don't we take my new car for a spin? There's a place I want to show you not too far from here. We can eat the cake there."

My guard came up. "I'm not sure that's a good idea." He reached out and put his hand on my arm. "Come

on, Rachel. Live a little for once. Life's not just about school and work, you know."

"It is for me," I said quietly.

"Well, it doesn't have to be. We won't be gone long. I promise."

It dawned on me that Mom wasn't expecting me home for at least another hour. It had been so slow all afternoon that I was able to finish cleaning up early.

"Okay," I said. "Let's go."

Sam zoomed down the street, showing off the speed of his Camaro.

"Slow down," I told him. "You'll get a ticket."

He laughed. "This car doesn't know how to go slow. Pretty awesome, huh?"

"It's a great car. You never told me where we're going, though."

"It's a surprise," he said. "You'll find out when we get there."

"I hate surprises," I said in a faraway voice that didn't sound like my own.

"Well, I think you'll like this one." Sam turned onto a side street that had river access. He drove down the windy road until he pulled up to a beautiful spot near the Sacramento River. No one else was around, and the only sound was the gentle gurgling of the water. The moonlight shining on the water seemed almost magical. "This is where I like to come when I want to be by myself—just to think."

"It's really nice," I said, taking it all in. I felt honored somehow that he wanted to share his special spot with me.

Sam jumped out of the car and came around to open the door for me. I stepped out slowly, trying to balance the cake in one hand. Then he grabbed a huge multicolored beach towel out of the back seat and laid it out on a sandy spot near the river bank. He sat down on the towel and patted the spot next to him.

"Let's sit over here."

I sat down beside him and pulled two plastic forks out of my pocket. I handed him one and kept the other for myself. "Well, I guess we should eat the cake while it's still nice and fresh. I hope you don't mind I brought two forks. Most people say a slice of cake is way too big for one person. Besides, it's the most amazing cake I've ever had. So, I guess you could say I had some selfish reasons for bringing it."

He grinned from ear to ear. "I knew this wasn't all about me and my birthday."

"Well, it's a good excuse, isn't it? Go ahead ... Dig in. You're the birthday boy."

He took a bite, savoring it for a long time. "I have to admit I thought you were just exaggerating, but this is the best cake I've ever had in my life."

"Told you so," I said, grabbing a quick bite of my own. We both sat there for a long time, looking out at the water and nibbling on the cake, lost in our own thoughts. "I'm sorry if I was rude to you the other day," I said finally. "I guess I just don't understand why you would be interested in me when you could probably be with any girl at school."

He finished chewing a bite of cake and said, "Most of them are shallow. I don't like girls who are shallow."

"How do you know I'm not? Shallow, I mean."

"I guess I just know. You may give off this tough girl act when you're around people, but I know there's a great girl in there, and I want to get to know you better. Is that such a crime?"

"No. I'm just not sure you'll like what you find."

Sam reached over and touched my hand, giving me goose bumps. "Let me be the judge of that, okay?"

"Okay."

"You know, I was thinking … You know a lot about my family already, but I don't know anything about yours."

"Not much to tell," I said with a shrug. "There's just me, my mom, and my sister."

Sam looked me in the eyes, like he already knew there was more to the story. "What about your dad? How did he die?"

I was taken aback, unable to speak. That was the one subject I was not prepared to talk about. "How did you know he died?"

"Some kids at school told me. I didn't think it was a big secret."

I cleared my throat before I continued. "It's not. It's just not something I like to talk about."

"You don't have to then," he said in a calm, even tone. "But when you're ready to talk about it, I'm here to listen." Something about Sam made me want to open up more.

I just wasn't sure how. I stared out at the water for a long time, trying to find the nerve to say more. Finally, I did.

"It was about ten years ago. I was seven at the time. My sister, Michelle, was just two. Our dad used to take us to band practice once a week. He was part of this classic rock band that played old eighties music, and Michelle and I loved to go and cheer him on. Mom never went, though. She always called it her time. Sometimes she would hang out with her friends; sometimes she would just stay home and take a long hot bath. I think she enjoyed the break, especially since Michelle was in the middle of the terrible twos.

"Anyway, we were on our way home from band practice that night. It was a dark, rainy night in January. Michelle was already passed out in her car seat. Dad and I were singing some old country song that was playing on the radio." It made me sad that I couldn't remember what song it was anymore. I took a deep breath before I continued.

"Dad always stopped on the way home to get me a cherry Icee from the convenience store. I asked him if we were going to get an Icee, and he rarely ever told me no. He was kind of a pushover about things like that. So, he pulled over right in front of the store, and he looked back at Michelle, who was sound asleep. He asked if I would watch her for a minute, and of course, I said yes. It made me feel like I was a big girl because he trusted me.

"So, Dad went into the store. There was a big window, so I could see him the whole time. He went to the Icee dispenser and started filling a cup. Then I noticed two men who went in right after him. They were wearing hoodies, so I couldn't really see their faces. I watched them walk around the store for a while, but it didn't seem like they were there to buy anything. And they weren't. They came to the cashier, and one of them, the taller one, whipped out a gun. He was yelling something at the cashier, an older Hispanic guy, and the cashier was frantically trying to open the register.

"My dad was watching all of this, and he was trying to make his way to the front of the store. But I could tell he was torn. He was the kind of person who liked to take matters into his own hands. I knew that he wasn't just going to let the guys take off with the money. I started feeling sick to my stomach. After the cashier had filled their bag with money, both of the guys tried to make a run for it.

"I could see Dad crouched down behind the cereal aisle, and he jumped out and grabbed the guy with the gun. He was trying to pull the gun from his hand. They fought and struggled for what seemed like a long time. And then there was a loud bang. It scared me and woke up Michelle. Now she was whaling like a banshee.

"I couldn't tell who had been shot at first, but then then both of the robbers ran off, and Dad was left lying there in a puddle of his own blood. I just sat there for a while. I guess I was paralyzed with fear. Then, when I could see that the robbers were long gone, I slowly unbuckled myself and walked up to my dad. The cashier was on the phone with the police, trying to get help, and other people were starting to gather around too. He didn't really look like himself. He was so pale, and there was so much blood. He looked up at me for a minute, like he was going to say something, but then he just closed his eyes. And that was it. He was gone."

I expected Sam to say something clever or maybe the generic I'm-so-sorry-for-your-loss statement that I had heard over a million times. But he didn't. He just sat there, staring out at the water.

Finally, he looked at me with pain in his eyes. "Did they ever catch those guys?"

I nodded. "Yes. The one who shot him got first-degree murder. I think he's still in jail. But the other one only got armed robbery, so he's been out for a while now. They could never pay enough, though. Because of them, Michelle and I have to live the rest of our lives without our dad."

"That must be rough," he said quietly.

I wiped a tear from my eye. "You have no idea how hard it is. I think about him all the time. It just doesn't seem fair, you know?"

"It's not fair," he agreed. "But it's also not your fault." A huge lump formed in my throat. That's what they used to tell me in counseling all the time. The truth was, I did blame myself for my father's death. If I hadn't begged for that Icee, he never would have gone into that store that night, and he never would have been shot. I felt the tears start to well up, and I tried to wipe them away with the back of my hand.

Sam just put his arm around me, and we stared out at the water. No words were needed. Just the fact that he was there with me said everything. I could have stayed there with Sam on that river bank forever, but I knew that moment couldn't last forever. I had to go back to the real world sometime, even if it wasn't the best world to go back to.

CHAPTER

8

I tiptoed into the house quietly that night, trying my best not to disturb anyone. I had almost made it to my room when I heard my mother clear her throat.

"Where were you tonight?" she mumbled under her breath.

I shrugged. "I told you. I had to work late."

"Stop lying!" she shouted. "I called Burger Shack, and there was no answer. Besides, even when you have the closing shift, you're never this late. So tell me the truth. Where were you tonight?"

"Out with a friend, okay?"

"No, it's not okay. You had the car all night, and I was worried. So was your sister."

"Sorry," I said sarcastically as I started to walk toward my room.

But Mom wouldn't let it go. She grabbed me by the arm, yanking me backward.

"You think sorry is enough?" she asked, shaking her head.

I yanked my arm out of her grip. "I shouldn't have to apologize for being a normal seventeen-year-old. Now, if you don't mind, I'm going to bed."

That was just enough to set her off, and she raised her arm and slapped me across the face. It stung, and I just stood there in shock, unable to move. Then her expression softened a bit.

"You know, Rachel, you had this great bond with your dad, but you've always been like a stranger to me. Have I really been that awful of a mother all these years?"

I shook my head. "No, you've just been hurting all these years. We all have, except Michelle is too young to remember, so I guess she thinks this is all normal."

She considered this for a minute. "Maybe she does. And maybe this is normal for us. All I know is your father was a better parent than me. He would have done anything for the two of you. I mean, he went into that store that night just because you wanted that damn Icee. It was freezing cold that night. Why did you want an Icee anyway?"

If words could kill, I would have died right there on the spot. She knew that was a sensitive subject for me, but she continued to bring it up.

"You're right about one thing," I said. "He was the better parent. And do you know why? Because he would have never said something like that to me. That's exactly why we've never been that close—because you say things like that. Well you know what, Mother? I wish it was you who died that day!"

With that, I stormed into my room without another word.

After I'd washed my face and slipped into some comfortable clothes, I crawled into bed, trying my best to drown out the sound of my mother's cruel words, but it was impossible.

Michelle sat up in bed, rubbing her eyes sleepily. "I heard you guys fighting."

"Sorry you had to hear that, kiddo. Try to get back to sleep."

I heard her lay back on her pillow and rustle around a bit before she turned toward me.

"It isn't fair that Mom always blames you because Dad went into the store that night. I mean, you were just a kid. It wasn't your fault."

I could hear Sam's voice saying those same words by the river just a few hours ago. For the first time, I really believed they were true.

"I know it wasn't my fault."

"So, where were you tonight, anyway?" Michelle asked through a yawn.

"None of your business."

She giggled with her trademark belly laugh. "You were with a boy, weren't you?"

I tossed a pillow at her. "So what if I was?"

"I knew it!" she squealed. "Is he cute?"

I pictured Sam with his mop of dark-blond hair, strong athletic body, and those amazing blue-green eyes that seemed to smile when he did. But I also knew there was much more to him than that. "I guess you could say he's good looking. But he's just a friend. I'm going to tutor him on Saturday if you want to come."

"Really? You'd let me come?"

"Sure, as long as you can stay out of the way. And try to keep your mouth shut." I knew my sister had a reputation for being a blabbermouth. When she was younger, it was embarrassing to take her out in public because she was always commenting people's appearance or things that were none of her business. One time, she asked an overweight man if he was pregnant. I was laughing inside, but I knew the man didn't think it was funny. I just apologized and took Michelle out of the store as quickly as possible, forgetting about the groceries we needed to buy.

"I'll behave. I promise."

I smiled. "Okay. Good night, Michelle."

"Good night."

CHAPTER

9

Michelle's eyes just about popped out of their sockets when we pulled up in front of Sam's house on Saturday afternoon.

"Your boyfriend lives here?"

"He's not my boyfriend," I corrected. "He's just a friend."

"But you like him, so he might be your boyfriend in the future. And if that doesn't work out, maybe he can be my boyfriend," she said with a giggle. "This place is awesome!"

"Yes, it is," I agreed, admiring the beautiful landscaping. Just then, Sam came out to greet us. He was wearing a light blue T-shirt and a pair of jeans, which, of course, looked amazing on him. He nodded at both of us and smiled.

Michelle's grin grew even bigger, and I just knew something embarrassing was about to come out of her mouth. Unfortunately, I was right.

"You're right, Rachel. He is smoking hot!"

Sam looked flattered at the compliment, but I wanted to strangle my little sister for being so blunt.

"Hi, Sam," I said. "This is my annoying kid sister, Michelle. Michelle, this is Sam."

Michelle shot me one of her poison dart looks before she turned to Sam. "Nice to meet you. I've heard lots of good things about you."

"That's good to hear," Sam said. "Shall we get started?" A little while later, Sam and I were sitting across from each other at the kitchen table, working on some geometry problems. Michelle was outside shooting some hoops on the basketball court, and I could hear the ball bouncing against the pavement. Every once in a while, Sam would look up from his paper with this dreamy look in his eyes.

"Would you stop looking at me that way? It makes it kind of hard to concentrate."

Sam shrugged. "I can't help it. You look really pretty today."

I was wearing one of my nicer outfits, which was a pale green button-up shirt and the only pair of jeans I owned that didn't have any holes. I'd also left my hair down instead of wearing it in my signature ponytail, which was a must on days I worked at Burger Shack. So for me, I guess I did look nice. But I still didn't hold a candle to Jessica Sinclair with her designer clothes and expensive haircuts by some famous hairdresser in the bay area. Not that it was a competition or anything, and I wouldn't want to be like her anyway. But I still couldn't understand why Sam seemed so interested in me, when there were so many girls out there who seemed like they were a way better fit for him. I didn't want to seem rude, so I thanked him for the compliment.

We worked quietly for a while before he looked up at me and said, "Thanks again for helping me out. I think I'm going to ace the test on Friday."

"No problem. Thanks for letting me bring Michelle." I looked over the problems he had finished. They were all correct, which made me wonder if he really needed a tutor at all.

"Yeah, she seems like a great kid."

I smiled. "She is, even if she has a big mouth sometimes." Sam took a drink of lemonade that the housekeeper had made for us. I'd never had lemonade that didn't come out of a box or can before, and it was really good. It even had little slices of lemon in it, which made it seem more refreshing. I took a drink from my own glass, savoring it. "You know," he said, "You really are lucky."

I looked around his beautiful home in disbelief. "You think *I'm* lucky?"

"Sure. I always wanted a sibling. I was lonely a lot when I was kid. I used to always beg my parents to have another baby. I even asked Santa for a few years until I figured out that just wasn't going to happen. A baby just didn't fit into my parents' lifestyle. I don't even think I was planned, and they sure couldn't wait until I got old enough that they could leave me on my own. So you are lucky to have a sister. I mean, friends will come and go, but you'll always have her—no matter what."

"I guess I never thought of it that way," I said quietly. I was starting to realize what a good friend Sam was and how lucky I was to have him in my life too. The wall I had built around myself was slowly starting to crumble, and that was exciting and scary all at once. I cleared my throat, wanting to change the subject. "I'm sorry if I was a little depressing the other night. I hadn't really talked about what happened that night for a long time."

Sam put his pencil down and looked up at me. "You weren't depressing at all. I wouldn't have asked if I didn't want to know. Right?"

"Right," I agreed. "It really meant a lot to me ... what you said."

Sam nodded, and I could tell he knew exactly what I was talking about. "I just told you the truth. It wasn't your fault. And I think your dad would want you to know that too."

When I was younger, I used to think that my dad's spirit was still with me, watching over me. I'd imagine how he would react to some of the things I did. Sometimes I could actually hear him giving me advice. But his voice just seemed to fade away as I got older. Sometimes I would give anything to hear him again, even if he was lecturing me about something I did wrong. But the rational side of me knew that was impossible. Still, another part of me wondered if he was right there with me sometimes, even if I couldn't see him.

"Sam," I said quietly. "Where do you think people go, you know, after they die?"

Sam bit his bottom lip. He seemed to be searching for the right words. "I guess we'll never know until we're gone. I just hope it's really nice—the kind of place where nobody has to be hurt or mad or sad. Everyone would be happy, and it would be like a never-ending party. I do believe there has to be more to it than just going to sleep and never waking up. What do you think, Rachel? Do you believe that a person's spirit lives on?"

I took a deep breath. That was a subject I had thought a lot about since my dad died, but I didn't have any clear-cut answers for. "I really don't know what I believe. I've always been a realist, so I guess it's hard for me to believe in anything I can't see or feel. For all I know, it's just like going to sleep."

Sam shook his head. "There's so much more to it."

"How do you know that?" I asked. "I mean, how can you be so sure?"

"I just know," he said with a confident shrug.

It seemed like he wanted to say more, but he was interrupted by his mother, who came bouncing into the kitchen pulling a suitcase behind her.

"We're home!" she announced in a cheerful voice, but her smile faded as soon as she saw me. "Oh, I didn't realize you had company."

"Mom, you're home early," Sam said, surprised.

She nodded. "We took an earlier flight. Your dad has a meeting first thing in the morning, so he wanted to rest up for that. I see the two of you are studying?"

"Yes," Sam said. "Rachel's helping me with math."

"Well that's good. You can never study too much."

"So how was your trip?" Sam asked, clearly wanting to change the subject.

"It was wonderful, but I'll tell you about it later. Right now, I think I will catch a nap before dinner. Why don't you tell Rosalee to whip up something Italian?" Then she cleared her throat before she asked, "Will your friend be joining us for dinner?"

It was obvious that the invite was more out of obligation, which made me feel uncomfortable. "I really should be getting home after this."

Mrs. Goodwin waved her hand in the air. "Don't be silly. You should stay."

"Yeah, you should stay," Sam agreed.

Before I had the chance to answer, Michelle came into the kitchen, dribbling a basketball. "Stay for what?"

Mrs. Goodwin looked surprised, and I realized she probably had no idea Michelle was there. She was also probably not too happy about a basketball being bounced around in the house. That was two strikes against us already.

"It doesn't matter because we really need to get home," I told her with a stern look that said, *You better keep your mouth shut, or else.*

Sam cleared his throat. "Mom, this is Rachel's sister, Michelle."

Michelle reached out her sweaty hand to Mrs. Goodwin. "Nice to meet you."

"Nice to meet you too," Mrs. Goodwin said, shaking her hand. "Shall we set the table for two more then?"

"Sure!" Michelle cheered. "We never turn down a free meal!"

I elbowed her in the ribs and narrowed my eyes at her in my best attempt at a warning. "I told you. We have to go." Michelle rolled her eyes, clearly oblivious to my warning stare. "What are we going to eat then? You know there's no food in the house."

Mrs. Goodwin looked surprised at Michelle's comment. "I insist, really."

"Yeah, we insist," Sam said with that dopey grin that was hard to say no to.

"All right, we'll stay."

"Yeah!" Michelle cheered, doing a little victory dance.

And I knew this was going to be a very long and awkward night.

I looked around nervously at the place settings with so many different forks. I had no idea which one to use first, so I just followed everyone's lead, using the smaller one for the salad. Mr. Goodwin sat across from me and hadn't said more than two words since he sat down for dinner. He was a tall man with slightly graying light brown hair, a narrow face and chin, and a mustache that seemed well groomed. He had a serious way about him, like you almost couldn't imagine him smiling. It almost seemed like he didn't go with the bubbly, energetic Mrs. Goodwin. Sam had told me he was a man of few words, but the silence made me feel even more uncomfortable. Luckily, Michelle made herself right at home, happily eating her salad and telling us about her school play at the same time.

"I get to wear this pretty pink dress, and the set looks like a real castle!" she said, with her mouth full of salad. I'd thought about telling her to chew with her mouth closed, but I didn't want to draw any more attention to it. "And the best part is, Rachel wrote this play when she was in middle school."

"That's really awesome," Sam said. "I used to love drama when I was in middle school. Maybe I could come watch the play?"

Michelle beamed. "You'd really come?"

"Of course," Sam answered. "We could make a night of it, maybe grab some dinner after."

He looked at me for approval, but all I could do was give him a nervous smile.

His mother cleared her throat and said, "We'll just have to see. If you're done with your schoolwork on time, then I guess that would be all right."

Sam bit his bottom lip, something I'd only seen him do when he was deep in thought or mad about something. From the look on his face, I guessed it was the latter.

"I didn't ask for your permission, Mom. I am eighteen now, remember?"

Mrs. Goodwin put her fork down and narrowed her eyes at him. "But you are still under our roof, and you'll abide by our rules."

Mr. Goodwin put his hand on her shoulder. "Now, Norma, don't embarrass Sam in front of his friends. Remember when we were eighteen? We didn't exactly do what our parents told us to either."

Her expression softened a bit, and for the first time, I saw that they actually did go together very well. They sort of balanced each other out in a way. Nobody said much for the rest of the meal, but it became more of a relaxed silence, and for the first time, I felt like I belonged at that table.

CHAPTER

10

For the next week, my life revolved around school and work. I'd picked up some extra hours at Burger Shack, which was a good thing because I needed the money. But I have to admit, I was a little jealous of the kids who would be going to a party on Friday night while I was covered in grease. Life seemed so easy for them.

On my way to world history, Sam came running up to me with a huge smile on his face. "Mark's having a party at his place Friday night. It sounds like a blast."

"I know. Everyone's talking about it."

"Well, do you want to go?"

I shook my head. "I can't. I have to work."

He rolled his eyes, clearly annoyed. "Can't you just take a night off? Have a little fun for once?"

"No, I can't," I said with a sigh.

"Why not?"

"Because I need the money!" I snapped. "Which is something you could never understand because you've never had that problem."

Sam's eyes flashed with something between hurt and anger, I'd never seen that look on his face before, and it scared me a little. "Do you really think my life is so easy just because my parents have money? Because nothing could be further from the truth. Sure, I never wanted for anything. But my nannies and chauffeurs know me better than my own two parents. That right there should tell you something." With that, he stomped off, leaving me speechless.

No matter how hard I tried to keep my mind on my job at Burger Shack, I couldn't stop thinking about Sam. I felt horrible about the way I had talked to him. He didn't choose his situation in life any more than I had chosen mine, and he'd only invited me to go to a party with him. He really didn't deserve the way that I had talked to him. I tried my best to keep my mind on my job, hoping to earn some tips. And then, just as I was cleaning up to go home for the day, there he was. Standing in the doorway, looking as handsome as ever. He looked sad, though.

"Hi, Rachel."

"Hey, Sam," I said, looking down at my feet. "I'm sorry about the way I talked to you earlier. I feel really bad about that."

He shrugged. "I feel bad about how I stomped off too. I should have been more understanding. So, I guess we're even?"

"I guess," I said, feeling relieved that he didn't seem mad at me.

Then a big smile spread across his face. "So, are you almost done here?"

I nodded. "I just have a few more things to check off my list before I can lock up."

"Is there anything I can do to help?"

I was taken aback by his offer, and stood there silently for a moment before I was able to speak. "Well you can make sure each table has enough napkins, salt, pepper and ketchup."

"He nodded. Got it. And after that, are you free?"

"I guess."

"Good."

Sam and I both finished up all the small things that needed to be done each night at closing time, and I made sure everything was locked up behind us.

"So, what do you have in mind?" I asked.

"You'll see," he told me as he opened the passenger door. "You know I don't like surprises," I told him as I sat

down in the car and buckled up. "Well, I think you'll like this one."

I just smiled and enjoyed the ride, while Sam drove down the familiar road that led to the river. He reached out and held my hand as we drove, and I suddenly felt all of the stress and tension I'd been holding in leave my body. The moon was full that night, leaving a beautiful glow over the water. In that moment, it felt like we were the only two people on Earth. And it still felt that way hours later, as we sat looking out at the river while time seemed to stand still.

"Thanks for bringing me here tonight," I told Sam as I leaned into him, taking in the aroma of his aftershave. "I really needed this."

"Me too," he said quietly. "I just couldn't stand the thought of things being weird between us, you know? It just didn't feel right."

I nodded. "I felt kind of off all afternoon. I couldn't stop thinking about how we left things."

"Well, things are great now," he said. "I guess that's what matters, right?"

"Right." I watched as a boat went zooming by and pretended not to notice when Sam pulled me a little closer.

"So, I guess your sister's play is coming up this weekend?" he asked casually.

"Yes, but I don't want you to feel obligated to come or anything. I mean, it was nice of you to offer, but—"

"No, I want to come. I wouldn't have offered if I didn't want to come," he said quickly. "Do you think your mom will be there?"

I shrugged. "I'm not sure. It depends on how she's feeling that day, I guess."

Sam nodded like he understood exactly what I was talking about. "I just thought it would be nice since I haven't met her yet."

You're not missing much, I thought to myself as I stared blankly out at the water.

"Do you think your dad would have come if he were still alive?" Sam asked.

"I know he would have come. He was the most awesome dad in the universe."

A knowing smile spread across Sam's face. "I know. I mean, I bet he was. Tell me about him. What was he like?"

"Well, it's getting harder and harder to remember those little details," I told him. "But my dad was kind and funny. He loved music. He was even in a band that played old eighties music. He played bass and guitar."

"Sounds like we would have gotten along great," Sam said. "I play a little too. I mean, I'm not in a band or anything, but I can figure out just about any song."

"Really?" I asked, surprised. "I didn't know you played."

"Well, my parents think it's a big waste of time, so I probably don't play as much as I'd like to."

"Who taught you then?" I asked, curious.

Sam bit his bottom lip, deep in thought. "I guess I just taught myself."

"Well, I'd love to hear you play sometime."

"You will."

Sam and I just sat in silence for a while, but it didn't feel strange or awkward. Somehow, it just felt right. And I don't remember exactly how that kiss started, but I do know it was one of those life-changing moments I will never forget. It was warm and gentle and loving—everything a kiss should be. I never wanted that moment to end, and I imagined that we were alone on a deserted island. But the real world was a far cry from my fantasy.

CHAPTER

11

From that moment on, Sam and I were pretty much inseparable. It became common news around campus that we were an item. Some people were happy for us.

Other people, like Jessica Sinclair, were less than enthusiastic. I tried my best to ignore all of the dirty looks and eye rolls that were directed toward me, but one day she pushed me way too far. As she walked past me in the hall with her groupies by her side, she elbowed me and knocked all of my books out of my arms, sending them flying in every direction.

"Sorry about that," she said with a smug look on her face.

I bent down and started picking up my books. "No you're not."

She ran her fingers through her long blonde hair. "So, I hear you and Sam are together."

I clutched my books closer to my chest. "Yeah. What's it to you?"

"Well, don't you think he should be with someone more ... his type?"

"Who says I'm not his type?" I asked, feeling the heat rise in my cheeks.

Jessica rolled her eyes. "You know what I mean."

"Yeah, I know what you mean, but I don't care. I feel sorry for people like you because you always want what you don't have. Even if Sam did like you, which he doesn't, you'd be tired of him in about a week because that's how people like you operate."

That seemed to enrage her, and she lunged after me and pinned me against the lockers. "Listen, lowlife. You need to crawl back under the rock you came from. And you know what? No one will even notice your gone."

Her hands were around my throat, and I was gasping for air. I tried with all of my might to push her away, but she was stronger than she looked. By this time, the whole school was gathered around, watching like we were some sort of spectator sport. I was starting to feel dizzy, like I might pass out. Then Sam came from out of nowhere and pulled Jessica off of me. He pinned her against the lockers with a look of rage in his eyes that I'd never seen before.

"What in the hell do you think you're doing? If you want to mess with her, you'll have to go through me first. Do you understand?"

There was fear in the eyes of Jessica Sinclair, and that was a really good feeling. Unfortunately, that feeling didn't last long because the principal, Mr. Wilson, came marching through the sea of people with a look of disapproval on his face. That look changed to something between shock and anger when he saw Sam with his hands around Jessica's throat.

"What is going on here?" He snapped.

"Let it go, Sam," I whispered, trying to calm him down. "It's not worth it."

Sam slowly loosened his grip on Jessica, which she used to her advantage.

"He just attacked me for no reason!" she shrieked, looking like a damsel in distress.

"In my office right now, Mr. Goodwin!" the principal snapped.

Sam hung his head and walked toward the office like a prisoner on his way to execution.

After school, I went looking for Sam, but he was nowhere to be found. I had this sinking feeling that something was very wrong, and that feeling was confirmed when Jessica came marching up to me with that smug look on her face.

"I heard your boyfriend was suspended for attacking me earlier," she sneered. "That really sucks for him because now he can't play in the tournament tomorrow night. Well, I sure hope he learned his lesson."

She marched off with her groupies without another word. Part of me was so angry I wanted to chase after her and punch that smile off of her face. Another part of me just felt awful that Sam was in trouble for defending me. It was like I had a curse that rubbed off on anyone I touched. Suddenly, I knew what I had to do. I got in my car and drove to Sam's house. I rang the doorbell three times before his mother finally answered. I could tell right away she was disappointed to see me.

"Hello, Rachel."

"Hi, Mrs. Goodwin. Is Sam at home?"

"Yes, he is, but I'm afraid you can't see him. He was suspended from school today, and we don't tolerate that type of behavior in this house. So, he's grounded until further notice."

"Well, the principal was being totally unfair," I told her. "He was just trying to defend me against that awful girl Jessica and—"

She waved her hand in the air to cut me off. "He told me exactly what happened."

I blinked. "He did?"

"Yes, and the simple truth of the matter is, I don't care *why* he was suspended. Why don't you come in and sit down, Rachel? I think it's time we had a little chat."

I silently followed her into the living room and sat across from her on the sofa. My palms were all sweaty, and my heart was pounding out of my chest. Something about Mrs. Goodwin made me feel uncomfortable, and it made it even worse that she seemed so calm cool and collected. The maid poured us some lemonade, and I sipped it slowly, trying to stall the conversation I knew was coming.

"So, you and Sam have been seeing a lot of each other?"

I nodded. "Yes. I've been helping him out with math. Plus, we enjoy spending time together."

"And you care about him?"

"Very much. Sam's a great guy. I guess you could say he's grown on me."

"Well, if you really do care about him as much as you say you do, then you'll do the right thing and stay away from him."

I nearly choked on my lemonade. "What?"

"Well, dear. This has nothing to do with you, really. Sam is going to college next year. He's already received three acceptance letters to very prestigious universities, all of which are out of state. He just needs to stay focused right now. He doesn't have time for any distractions. Do I make myself clear?"

I wanted to say so many things at the moment, but the only thing I could do was nod.

A smile spread across Mrs. Goodwin's face. "I'm glad we have an understanding. This is for your own good really. I wouldn't want to see you get hurt when he moves away this summer. It's just not the right time for a serious relationship for either of you. Senior year is hard enough without adding that to the mix, so it's best to just nip things in the bud before it gets too serious."

"There's just one more thing," I said. "Do you think I could see him, just for a minute? I brought his homework."

She bit her bottom lip. "Okay, but make it quick."

As I walked upstairs to Sam's room, I felt on the verge of tears. Sam was my best friend—my only friend. I felt like I would be ending something that was just beginning. But deep down, I knew Mrs. Goodwin was right. I would only be holding him back. He would be going to college, and I didn't even know for sure what I would be doing after high school. So, I had to do the right thing, even if it killed me. I took a deep breath before I knocked on the door.

"Who is it?" I heard him mumble from the other side of the door.

"It's me, Rachel."

Within seconds, he opened the door and threw his arms around me. I could already tell, he wasn't going to make this easy.

"It's so good to see you," he whispered in my ear, and then he kissed me.

For a few weak seconds, I kissed him back. But then I remembered what Mrs. Goodwin had said, and I snapped back into reality. When I pulled away from him, I knew that he could tell something was wrong.

"What's going on?" he asked.

"I just came to bring your homework and to thank you for what you did for me today. Nobody's ever done anything like that for me before."

He narrowed his eyes. "Why do I feel a *but* coming on?"

"But I don't think it's a good idea for us to keep seeing each other."

His eyes flashed with anger. "My mom put you up to this, didn't she?"

"I talked to her, but I do think she made some valid points. You're going to college. It's just not a good time for a relationship. I mean, I tried to tell you that from the beginning, but you wouldn't listen."

"I know you felt something too," Sam pleaded.

I looked down at my feet, trying to avoid eye contact. "Maybe I did, but that doesn't make it right."

"I don't agree with you. Something really awesome was starting between us, and you're just too chicken to give it a chance. What happened to the girl I met who didn't listen to anyone's opinions? You think for yourself. That's one of the things I like about you."

"I'm just being realistic," I told him. "I'll see you around school, but that's it. I don't think it's a good idea for me to tutor you anymore either."

He sighed. "Fine, but at least let me give you this." He reached into his backpack and pulled out a check, and then he handed it to me.

I looked at the amount, and my eyes just about popped out of my head. "This is more than you owe me."

"It's for all of next week too," he explained.

"Well, I don't want your money."

I handed him the check and walked out without looking back.

CHAPTER

12

"Hold still, or I'm going to smear your mascara," I told Michelle as I helped her get ready for the play. She looked at herself in the mirror and beamed.

"Wow, this looks great! You should really think about being a makeup artist. Maybe you could do makeup for the stars!"

"I'd love that, but I looked up the price of beauty school, and it's totally out of our budget."

Michelle twisted her hair into a bun and made a silly face in the mirror. "Well, at least you have the extra money from tutoring Sam."

"Not anymore," I said.

"Why not?"

"Because our lives are just going separate ways. I decided it was the best thing for both of us if we stopped seeing each other now—before things got too serious."

Michelle frowned. "That sounds more like Mrs. Goodwin talking. I could tell you really liked him."

"That's exactly why I had to break things off with him," I explained.

"So, does this mean he's not coming to the play tonight?"

"Yes. It means he won't be coming."

"Well, is Mom coming at least?" she asked with a sigh. I knew that wasn't very likely because I hadn't even seen her all day. I was so angry that she made no effort even though the flyer for the play had been on the fridge for a month. But I knew it would mean a lot to Michelle if I at least tried to get her to go.

I slowly opened the door to Mom's room. She was curled up in the same position she was the day before, wearing the same pair of pajamas. I could tell getting her up and ready in an hour just wasn't going to happen.

"Hey, Mom, are you coming to the play?" I was nearly shouting in an effort to get her attention.

She just rolled over and groaned.

"*Mom!*" This time, I was yelling at the top of my lungs. "You really are the worst mother on the planet. You know that?" I stomped out of the room and slammed the door behind me.

"Sorry, kiddo. Mom's a no-go," I told Michelle.

She couldn't hide her disappointment. "That figures."

"Hey, at least you have me. Let me just finish your hair, okay?"

I started working on her hair, putting it in a bun with little wisps of hair on each side. When I was done, she did a little twirl. I'd never seen her look so grown-up, and I'd never felt so proud. Just then, I could hear music playing outside.

"What's that?" Michelle asked.

I shrugged. "Probably just somebody's car radio."

"It sounds way too real to be a radio," she said as she darted toward the window. Then she giggled. "It's your boyfriend!"

My heart started pounding fast. "What?"

"Take a look."

I walked over to the window. Sure enough, Sam was strumming his guitar and singing the song "Heaven" by Bryan Adams. He was entranced in his own world as he sang. I could tell that every word of that song was for me. He was dressed in a suit and tie. He'd never looked or sounded so good.

"I'm going out there," I told Michelle.

He stopped singing when he saw that I was standing right in front of him, but he kept strumming the guitar.

I crossed my arms over my chest. "What are you doing here?"

He grinned. "I told you you'd hear me play sometime."

"Well, you sound great, but this still doesn't change anything."

He frowned. "Really?"

"Really. The fact is, you're still leaving this summer. And your Mom isn't going to make things easy."

"The best things in life aren't easy," he argued. "But they're so worth it. Maybe my parents want me to go to one of those colleges, but maybe that's not what I want. What I want is you."

"You're impossible, you know that?" I teased.

"Yeah, I know. I want to show you something, okay?" Sam led me to the parking lot behind our apartment complex, and I couldn't believe my eyes. My dad's '66 Chevy Chevelle was parked right in front of me. He loved that car almost as much as he loved us. I think it was so special to him because his dad had bought it for him. He even named it Grace. So many memories were made in the back seat of that car. Some were good, and others were bad. It was also the car we were driving on that horrible night.

In its day, it was shiny and red, and beautiful. It even seemed to have a personality all its own. But it had been under a cover in that parking lot for years. It needed more repairs than we could afford. It broke my heart that it was just collecting dust, but there wasn't much I could do about it.

"What did you do?" I asked, shocked. Sam looked at the car proudly. "I fixed it."

"But how?"

Sam put his finger on my lips. "Don't worry about how. I thought maybe we could drive it to the play? Then maybe to dinner after? I have reservations at this really great restaurant. You're going to love it."

I shook my head. "Your mom isn't going to like that."

"My parents are out of town for a business meeting. Besides, I didn't dress up for nothing, so …"

"So what?"

"Let's go."

CHAPTER

13

Everything about that night was amazing. The play was beautiful, and Michelle really nailed her part. I think her confidence had a lot to do with Sam. It meant a lot to her that he'd come, and it meant a lot to me too. I was starting to realize that Sam wasn't someone I could give up, even if I wanted to. He was part of me. I had no idea what the future might hold for either of us, but I knew one thing. I wanted it to be with him. Maybe it would be hard, but he was worth it.

After the play, Sam took us to a beautiful Italian restaurant where I had my first full meal in weeks. I almost hyperventilated when I saw the prices on the menu, but Sam insisted that it was on him. He told me to consider it payment for the tutoring since I wouldn't take the check. Of course, Michelle didn't let us get a word in during dinner. She talked about the play, about the kids at school, and about how delicious the food was. She must have commented on the food at least a dozen times. She always had been a bottomless pit.

As I drove my dad's old car home that night, I was full of so many emotions that I couldn't even describe. It brought back so many memories, and it felt like he was right there with me. I was so amazed by it all that I didn't even think to ask Sam how he had the keys and managed to fix a car that had more things wrong with it than I could count. But somehow, none of that seemed to matter. The three of us were driving along, listening to some classic tunes on the radio, singing, laughing, and having the time of our lives. When they played the song "Heaven," Sam reached over and took my hand in his, and all seemed right with the world.

When we pulled up to our apartment, Michelle jumped out of the car to tell Mom about the play. It always amazed me that no matter how horrible our mother was, Michelle never seemed to have any anger or resentment. She always just saw her as Mom.

"That was a great night," I said.

"Yes, it was," Sam agreed. "Michelle really is a great kid. But you know what the best part was?"

"What?"

"Seeing the look on your face when you saw the car. I wish I'd had a camera. It was priceless."

I beamed. "So how did you do it, anyway? I mean, that car had so many things wrong with it. And it couldn't have been easy to find the parts."

He shrugged. "I told you not to worry about that. Just enjoy the car, okay?"

"Okay," I agreed.

"So, I wanted to ask you something." Sam looked at me, curious. "Did you really write that play when you were in middle school? Because it was really good."

I nodded. "I used to really love drama, and writing helped keep my mind off of things. It's nothing, really."

"Nothing? It was great, and that's really cool that they still use it for a middle school play. You have a lot of talent. Don't sell yourself short. So, was the girl in the play supposed to be you?"

I shrugged. "I guess she's who I wanted to be."

"Well, I don't want you to be anyone except yourself," he whispered. Then he kissed me, and I kissed him back.

"So, does this mean I won that bet?" Sam asked, hopefully.

I'd almost forgotten about that bet on the first week of school. It seemed like it was so long ago now.

"You won the bet," I told him. "I can't get enough of you. There's no denying that. But I still don't know how this is all going to work out. I mean, I already promised your mother I would stay away from you."

He put his finger on my lips. "Let me handle her, okay?"

I nodded. "I just wish it didn't have to be so hard, you know?"

He shrugged. "It's more fun this way. Forbidden love, like Romeo and Juliet."

I laughed so hard I almost choked. "They both died, you know."

"Yeah, maybe that was a bad choice," he said. "We'll make up our own story as we go along—one with a happy ending."

"I can't wait," I told him.

"Me neither."

We kissed, and out of the corner of my eye, I saw Michelle looking out through the window, giving us the thumbs up. And I knew that someone was on our side.

CHAPTER

14

I think the fact that Sam and I were forbidden to see each other made me want him even more. We snuck in time together whenever we could, mostly at the river, which had become our spot. We spent my birthday there, enjoying the famous chocolate cake from Burger Shack and talking until we realized how late it was. He came back to school the following week, much to the disappointment of his mother. She tried to enroll him in a different school, probably to keep us away from each other. Lucky for us, there weren't any openings.

I had always been a straight A student, but trying to balance my relationship with Sam along with work and taking care of Michelle had taken a toll on my grades. My teachers all noticed the decline in my school performance. They lectured me about how much potential I had, how lucky I was to be going to Bright Academy, and how my scholarship could be taken away if things didn't improve. All of this went in one ear and out the other. All I could really think about was spending time with Sam.

One day after school we came back to my place. Sam had wanted to meet my mom for a while, but I kept putting it off for obvious reasons. I finally agreed to bring him home with me, mostly because we couldn't go to his house, and because it was raining that day, we couldn't hang out at the river either. I secretly hoped that she was passed out in her room, but no such luck. She was standing in the kitchen, making a salad. And she was wearing a leopard-print dress that was more appropriate for a twenty-year-old.

"Rachel, you're home!" she chirped. Her eyes seemed to be jumping all over the place. She was obviously high on something. "And you brought a friend."

I felt my throat tighten up. "Mom, this is Sam. Sam, this is my mom, Anna."

"Nice to meet you," Sam Said, reaching out to shake her hand.

She beamed. "Are you the Sam who fixed our car?"

"That's me," Sam said, proudly.

"Well then, you have to join us for dinner. It's the least I can do after everything you've done for us. I'm making lasagna."

Just then, Michelle ran out of our room and tackled Sam with a hug. "Yeah, Sam, you have to stay for dinner!" she chimed in, with a pleading look in her eyes.

"Well, since you put it that way, I'd love to stay," he said, tussling her hair.

All of a sudden, I felt like I was going to hyperventilate. The thought of having my mother and Sam at the same table eating dinner was just too much to process. What if she went on one of her drug-induced tirades? What would Sam think of me? I ran out to the back patio to get some air. Sam followed me a few minutes later.

"Rachel, what's going on?"

"I just had to get out of there," I said quickly.

He looked confused. "You don't want me to stay for dinner?"

"It's not that. It's just, my mom. She's so—"

"She seems nice to me," he said, finishing my sentence.

"She's a drug addict!" I snapped. "She might seem fine now, but she's a ticking time bomb ready to explode any minute. And I'm the one who's always left putting out the fires. Sometimes I feel like I'm barely hanging on by a thread, like there isn't much of me left to give. Is that the kind of person you want to be with? Because you have my permission to bail anytime. I'm not worth it, Sam. I'm broken."

Tears were streaming down my face. I thought to myself that Sam would be better off without me. But instead of running away, he just wiped away my tears and wrapped his arms around me.

"I'm not going anywhere," he assured me. "And you are not broken. You're one of the strongest people I've ever met. Your mom's drug problem doesn't have to define you. I just wish you could see yourself the way I see you. Because you're pretty damn awesome if you ask me."

I melted into him. "How do you always know how to make me feel better?"

"I don't know. I just do. Now, why don't we go see if we can help out in the kitchen?"

That night ended up being one of the best nights ever. Because mom was having one of her good days, she talked and laughed with us as we ate. The food was amazing, and I could tell she was proud of herself. I knew she was only on her best behavior because Sam was there, and I knew it probably wouldn't last. But that didn't matter. It just felt good to be like any other family. It felt almost normal.

CHAPTER

15

Sam and I grew closer every day, both physically and emotionally. It drove Jessica crazy to see us walking around school holding hands or making out by my car. I have to admit I enjoyed rubbing our relationship in her face a little too much sometimes. I would pour on the PDA whenever I knew she would see us and laugh about it afterward. Maybe that made me a mean girl, but I didn't care. What goes around comes around.

Even though I felt like I knew everything there was to know about Sam, there was still this mysterious side to him that I couldn't quite put my finger on. I could never figure out what it might be until the night by the river when everything changed. It was colder now, so we were bundled up, looking out at the water. Sam brought his guitar, and he'd been strumming it softly. Then he started to sing a beautiful song.

> You are my breath; you are my life.
> Anything I'd sacrifice
> just to see your face,

feel your warm embrace.
I want my life to be with you,
and I hope you feel it too.
You are the only one for me
Can't you see?
Can't you see?
You and me together
from now until forever.
That's how it's got to be.

I sat back, letting the words soak in for a minute. They sounded vaguely familiar, but I didn't know why. And then it hit me. I jumped up, my heart pounding.

"How did you know that song?"

Sam looked truly shocked. "What do you mean?"

"That's the song my dad used to sing to my mom.

Nobody else knew that song. He wrote it just for her. He was never very good with words, so he sang them. That was his way of telling her he loved her. And come to think of it, you know a lot of things that you could have no way of knowing. How did you know where the keys were to my Dad's old Chevy? How did you even know we owned that car? I never told you about it. And how come you always talk about him like you knew him?"

Sam froze. "I wish I could tell you, but I can't."

"Why not?"

"Because you probably wouldn't believe me anyway."

"Try me."

Sam just stared at his feet. "It's not that simple."

I crossed my arms over my chest because I was both cold and angry. "Well, if you can't trust me enough to tell me whatever it is you've been keeping from me, then I guess we don't have much of a relationship anyway."

Sam's face sank into a truly heartbroken expression. "Don't say that, Rachel."

"Well, it's the truth," I said. "I want a relationship built on honesty and trust, and you obviously don't trust me."

"I do, it's just …"

"Just what?"

"This isn't the kind of thing I can just blurt out."

I crossed my arms over my chest. "Take all the time you need."

We both stared out at the water until Sam was ready to talk.

"You have to promise me something first. Promise you'll keep an open mind because this is huge. And promise that this will stay between you and me."

I nodded. "I promise. Whatever it is, you can tell me."

Sam paused, making little circles in the sand with his foot. "There's something about myself that I've never told anyone, and I want to tell you, but this is really hard— harder than I thought it would be. You see, I was always different from other kids. I knew things that they didn't know, and I could see things that no one else could see."

"Like what?" I asked, curious.

"Like dead people."

I could feel my jaw drop. "You see dead people?"

He nodded. "Yes, I always have. I guess I'm what they call a medium. At first, I was afraid. Everyone thought I was strange because I seemed to be talking to nobody. My dad even took me to a child psychologist for a while and made me take some antipsychotic drug, but they wouldn't go away. And then, as I got older, I figured out that I could help them. Most of them are just stuck here because they have some sort of unfinished business. And if they take care of it, they can cross over."

"Cross over?" I repeated, trying to let it all sink in. He nodded. "You know, go through the light … to heaven, to be with the others."

"So how many of these people have you helped?" I asked, trying to keep an open mind.

"More than I can count." He looked at me, trying to read my expression. "You don't believe me, do you?"

"I want to, but it's hard. It goes against everything I've always believed. So, these people are all around us?"

He nodded. "Yes. Most of the time I only see them for a short time before they go where they're supposed to go. But there's this one guy who's been hanging around for a long time. He's worried about his family. He's mostly worried about you. He doesn't want you to blame yourself for what happened that night."

All of a sudden, I felt dizzy. "My Dad?"

"Yeah," Sam whispered. "He came to me about a year and a half ago. He'd been watching you guys, and it broke his heart to see you blaming yourself and your mom turning to drugs. But he didn't know what to do about it. Nobody else could see or hear him. Then he bumped into me, and we hit it off right away. Your dad is a really great guy. He's the one who taught me to play the guitar. He's funny too, but his cheesy jokes do get a little annoying sometimes." He looked up. "No offense, Fred."

"He's here right now?" I asked, dumbfounded. "Yes, he is. Do you want to say anything to him?"

I shook my head. "No. I can't say anything to my dad because he's dead. There has to be some other explanation for all of this."

Sam sighed. "I wish there was. You have to believe I'm telling you the truth. I wouldn't lie about something like this. As soon as he knows everything's okay, he can cross over."

I felt the heat rise in my cheeks. "That's the only reason you talked to me, isn't it? You didn't really like me. You just wanted my help crossing over my dead dad."

"Maybe at first it was like that," he admitted. "But once I got to know you, I really did like you. I still do. You have to believe that."

I bit my bottom lip. "I don't have to believe anything. I know I promised I would try to keep an open mind, but this is just too much to take in all at once. I'm going to need some time."

He nodded. "I understand. But you believe me, right?"

"I don't know what I believe, but I wish you'd kept it to yourself."

I turned and walked away without looking back.

CHAPTER

16

I've always thought that life was simple. Black or white with no room for shades of gray. What Sam told me tested my beliefs about everything, and that was a lot to take in all at once. If what Sam was saying was the truth, my dad had been watching us since he died, and he was worried about us. He couldn't even enjoy his afterlife, and I felt like that was all my fault.

I can still remember so many things about my dad. I remember how he used to scoop me up in his arms when he came home from work and how safe and protected I felt. I remember making pancakes together on Saturday mornings and how Mom would get mad because we made a mess in the kitchen. I remember the scent of his aftershave. I still kept a bottle on my bedside table. Those are all simple things, but they are all memories I hold close to my heart. That's how I wanted to remember my dad—full of life, not some ghostly spirit that I can't even see.

Burger Shack was crazy busy like usual on Friday, but my mind was somewhere else. My boss even noticed. Mr.

Thompson was a sweet man, chubby and round with a bald head and a thick gray beard. Everyone loved him. He was probably old enough to retire, but he loved working so much he had no plans to stop anytime soon. He was always positive and upbeat, so I knew something was wrong when he stomped over to me with a stern look on his face.

"Is everything okay, Rachel?"

I straightened my apron. "Yeah, why wouldn't it be?"

"Well, you forgot to bring table 3 her Coke, and table 6 is still waiting on their fries. It's just not like you. You're usually so on top of things."

"Sorry, I've just got a lot on my mind. I'll get right on it." I sprinted back to the kitchen, trying to make up for lost time. As I brought out the fries and Coke, I saw Jessica and her crew sitting at a table by the window, snickering and laughing. I didn't have to guess what they were laughing about. I knew it was probably about me.

"Hey, Rachel, aren't you going to take my order?" Jessica asked impatiently.

I dropped two more orders off before I finally came to take their order.

"It's about time," Jessica said.

I shrugged. "We're busy today. What do you want?" Jessica put her menu down and looked at me with cold blue eyes. "Actually, we're not that hungry anymore. We're going take our business somewhere else. But I do want to tell you something. I ran into Sam's mom at the store the other day. I casually mentioned what a cute couple you and Sam are, and she seemed surprised. Apparently, Sam isn't even supposed to be hanging out with you."

I felt the heat start to rise in my cheeks. "So what? Why don't you mind your own business? Is your life really that bad that you have to pry into mine?"

Jessica smiled her smug little smile. "I don't care that you're seeing Sam anymore, honestly. I have a new boyfriend. I've been seeing Todd Davis, captain of the football team. You can keep living your little fantasy life with Sam, but there's one more thing you should know. Sam gets a monthly allowance from his dad's company. That's been common knowledge since middle school. Now that his mom knows about your little secret they will probably cut him off. That means no more fancy dinners and gifts for you. It also means a major lifestyle change for Sam. Now I know money isn't everything, but don't you think Sam's going to resent that a little bit? Do you really think that's fair to him? To lose everything he has because of you?"

All of a sudden, my throat felt tight. I didn't have any snappy comeback, but when Jessica started laughing again, the rage that was brewing in me finally came out, and I slapped her across the face.

"You don't know anything about Sam!" I screamed. It was then that I realized everyone's eyes were on me, including Mr. Thompson's. As soon as my attention was somewhere else, Jessica lunged after me, pushing me against the wall. I pushed her back but even harder. It was then that Sam jumped in between us from out of nowhere.

"Come on, Rachel. She's not worth it. She's just trying to fire you up. don't give her the pleasure. Let's go out front and talk for a minute, okay?"

I let out a breath that I didn't even know I was holding. "There's nothing to talk about, Sam. Just leave me alone!" Sam winced, like my words had physically hurt him, while Jessica laughed.

"Uh-oh, looks like there's trouble in paradise," Jessica said with a satisfied smirk on her face. "Come on, girls. Let's go find another pace to eat. The service here is really slow." Jessica's friends followed her out of the restaurant like they were under some sort of spell, and I turned toward Sam, not sure what to say.

"Just give me five minutes," he pleaded with a look in his eyes that made it hard to say no.

"All right. Just let me get someone to take care of my customers."

⁂

As Sam and I stood outside with cars whizzing by, he seemed almost like a stranger to me, and I wondered if I ever really knew him at all and what other secrets he might be keeping from me. Part of me wished I'd never met him and that life could go back to what it was before. At the same time, I couldn't just forget how close we'd become in the last few months, leaving me feeling more conflicted than ever.

"So, what did Jessica say that got you so fired up?" Sam finally asked. "You seriously looked like you wanted to kill her."

I shrugged. "She was just stirring things up like she loves to do. I don't know why I let it get to me so much."

He nodded. "She's good at that. Did it have anything to do with me?"

I told him what Jessica had told me about running into his mom at the store and the conversation they'd had. When I was finished, he laughed.

"I doubt that's even true. My mom never goes to the store, she sends Rosalee with a very detailed list. And if she had talked to Jessica, I'm sure she would have told me. Jessica was just trying to get to you."

"I'm sure you're right," I agreed.

His expression turned more serious. "Listen, Rachel. I really need you to know I was telling you the truth yesterday. I know it's a lot to take in. I'm the one living it, and I can hardly believe it sometimes. Your dad wanted me to tell you a few things so you would know this is the real deal."

When I didn't answer, he continued.

"That song you were listening to on the night he died, he says it was 'I Think about You.' He says you two used to sing that song together all the time."

Suddenly, I was flooded with memories of my dad and me. That song began to play in my head, and I realized I hadn't mentioned it to Sam.

Sam cleared his throat and looked me right in the eyes. "He also told me what he was trying to tell you before he died. He says he was trying to sing a song that the two of you used to sing every night at bedtime. He could tell you were upset, and he wanted to calm you down. The song went something like this, 'I love you in the morning and in the afternoon. I love you in the evening and underneath the moon.'"

I could hear my Dad singing that song, clear as a bell, and I knew that Sam wasn't making this up. These were all things that were just between me and my dad. These were things he would have no way of knowing unless my father had told him. Although I believed Sam, I still had no idea what to say. But before I had the chance to say anything, there was a huge bang that came from Burger Shack. I could feel the heat blowing toward me, and I could hear people screaming inside.

I grabbed hold of Sam's arm and watched in disbelief as people scrambled from the building. "What happened?"

Sam shrugged. "I don't know."

My coworker Tracy ran toward us, coughing and gasping for air. "There was some sort of explosion in there! People are trapped, and some are hurt!"

Without even thinking, I ran into Burger Shack. As soon as I entered the building, I was hit with a wall of heat. I had to climb over a mountain of debris before I could get to anyone. Flames seemed to be growing by the minute. My eyes were watering, but I saw Mr. Thompson lying on the ground unconscious. I tried to get him to wake up, but it was no use.

"Rachel, are you crazy?" Sam shrieked as he ran in after me. "It's not safe to be in here! Tracy already called the fire department. They should be here any minute."

"By then it might be too late!" I told him. The flames seemed to be growing by the second.

Sam looked down at Mr. Thompson, who was lifeless. "All right, I'll help you get him out. But leave the rest to the paramedics, okay?"

I nodded, and Sam and I worked together to lift Mr. Thompson. He grabbed under his arms, and I held his feet. The smoke was making it hard to breathe, and we were both coughing. We finally managed to pull him out of the building and lay him on a grassy spot near the parking lot. I let out a sigh of relief and sat down beside him. But then I could hear the terrified screams of a small child inside.

"There's a kid in there!" I heard someone say, and without even thinking, I dashed back into the building.

The flames were getting larger now, and it was hard to see. But I could hear someone crying, and I followed the sound until I found a little girl, about five or six, under one of the tables.

"Hi, sweetie," I said. "Don't be afraid. I'm here to help you. My name's Rachel. What's your name?"

"Kristen," she said through her tears.

"Okay, Kristen, I need you to come to me. I'm going to get you out of here."

"I'm scared!" she sobbed.

"I know," I told her. "But you have to trust me." Slowly but surely, she crawled out from under the table, and I scooped her up in my arms. Now it was almost impossible to see anything, but I felt my way toward the door. Sam was standing in the doorway, frantically calling for me.

"Rachel, are you crazy? I told you to wait for help to come!"

"I couldn't just leave her!" I said.

Sam looked at the little girl, and his expression softened a bit. "Let's get you out of here, okay?"

He grabbed hold of my arm and led us both out of the building. But even after we were all safely outside, Kristen's sobs only got louder.

"It's okay," I told her. "You're safe now."

She was crying so hard now, it made it hard to understand her when she cried out, "My mom's still in there!"

I looked at the fear on the face of the little girl. I didn't want any child to feel the way I had when my dad died.

Then I looked up at Sam, who was already shaking his head.

"No, we can't go back in for her mom! That whole place will be up in flames any minute now."

"That's exactly why we have to! It might be too late by the time help gets here."

Just then, Jessica Sinclair came running up to us, her face as white as a ghost.

"What happened? I was just walking by, and I saw all the commotion."

As much as I hated Jessica, in that moment, all of those feelings were tossed aside. "There was some sort of explosion," I told her. "Can you take Kristen for a minute? I'm going back in there for her mom."

Jessica nodded and held out her arms as I handed over the little girl.

"Do you remember what your mom was wearing?" I asked.

Kristen nodded. "A pink sweater and some jeans. Promise you'll save my mommy. Please!"

"I promise I'll do my best," I said.

Sam let out an exasperated sigh. "Well if you're going back in there, so am I."

I was running on pure adrenalin as Sam and I ran into the building for the third time. It was now almost impossible to see anything, and it felt like my skin was on fire. My eyes burned, and Sam and I were both coughing uncontrollably from all of the smoke. But I had a one-track mind. I had to save Kristen's mom.

Through all of the smoke, I could vaguely make out the silhouette of a woman trapped under an overturned table, unconscious. And she was wearing a pink sweater.

"I think that's her!" I told Sam.

He nodded. "Yeah, but she doesn't look good. Help me pull the table off of her."

Sam and I worked together and pulled the table up and pushed it to the side. He was right. She didn't look good at all. Sam and I worked like a well-oiled machine as we carefully lifted her and started back toward the door. But this time, there were flames blocking the way. My heart started pounding fast when I realized we were trapped.

"Is there a back door?" Sam asked.

I opened my eyes enough to see that flames were blocking that exit too.

Suddenly, there was another loud bang, and that's when everything went black.

CHAPTER

17

The next thing I can remember I was straining to open my eyes. Something that I took for granted seemed to take so much effort. Every part of my body hurt, but I couldn't for the life of me remember why. I was finally able to focus enough to make out the blurry silhouettes of my mom and Michelle sitting beside me. Then I struggled some more until I was able to talk in a hoarse voice that didn't even sound like my own.

"Where am I?"

My mom bent down and brushed my hair away from my face. "You're in the hospital, sweetie. There was an explosion at Burger Shack. I'm so glad you're awake. You gave us a big scare."

All of a sudden, it started to come back to me. The explosion, the fire, me and Sam trying to pull Kristen's mom from the fire.

"Sam, is he okay?"

My mother bit her bottom lip. "We don't know yet, Rachel. When you were trying to get out of the building, a light fixture fell on all three of you. The woman Sam was pulling out is all right other than a nasty bump on her head and some smoke inhalation. Sam took the worst of it, I'm afraid. He's in the ICU in a coma."

"A coma?" I repeated, trying to let the severity of the situation sink in.

Michelle squeezed my hand. "He'll be all right. This is Sam were talking about. He's practically a superhero. Right now, you should just worry about getting better yourself. You need to rest."

Mom nodded in agreement. "She's right. Your health is the most important thing right now. They probably wouldn't let you in to see Sam anyway. Only immediate family is allowed in the ICU." Then she reached into her purse and grabbed some change, which she handed to Michelle. "Michelle, why don't you go to the waiting room and get yourself a snack from the vending machine. I'd like to talk to Rachel alone for a minute if you don't mind."

Michelle shrugged. "All right. I'm glad you're going to be okay, Rachel."

I tried to force a smile. "Me too, squirt."

Michelle walked off to the waiting room, leaving Mom and me sitting in awkward silence for a minute. Then she wiped a tear from her eye and started to talk.

"I want you to know that this accident was a big eye-opener for me. When I found out you were hurt and pictured what my life would be like without you or Michelle, I realized how wrong I've been. My priorities have been all screwed up, but I want you to know I'm ready to make a change."

I rolled my eyes. "I've heard that before."

She looked me in the eyes, and I could tell she was serious. Something about her was different.

"I mean it this time, Rachel. Things are going to change, but I can't do it on my own. I've called a treatment facility, and they have room to take me tomorrow."

"Tomorrow?" I repeated.

She nodded. "I've already called your grandmother, and she can stay with you girls while I'm gone. I don't know how long I will need to be in rehab. That depends on a lot of factors. But the important thing is, this is a turning point for our family. I promise you I will do whatever it takes to get better."

I was shocked and amazed all at once. I started to say something, but I realized no words were needed. Mom and I hugged and cried for a long time, and for the first time in a long time, I got a glimpse of the mom I thought I'd lost years ago. And that was the best feeling in the world.

CHAPTER

18

I learned right away that hospitals aren't the place to be if you want to get some sleep. Mom and Michelle went home for the night, promising to return first thing in the morning. Doctors and nurses came in to check on me every few hours, but even if they didn't come in, I'm sure I would have been lying there thinking about Sam. I tried to turn on the TV to distract myself, but the only thing that seemed to be on was the explosion at Burger Shack. The news reporter said they would be investigating the cause of the explosion, weather it was accidental or intentional. I wondered who would do something like that and why.

Finally, after a restless night, I couldn't take it anymore. I had to see Sam for myself. It was early in the morning, so the day-shift nurses wouldn't be by for an hour or so. It was the perfect time to sneak down to the ICU. I pulled the oxygen tube out of my nose and dragged myself out of bed and to the door, which made me feel like I was seventy instead of seventeen. But

I managed to do it, and before I knew it, I was across the hall in the elevator, headed for the third floor.

The ICU was eerily quiet, and there was only one nurse sitting at the station, an African American woman who looked to be in her mid-forties with long hair that she wore in a braid. There were double doors, which I knew led to the patient rooms, and there was a keypad to the right of the doors. I sat watching as the nurse typed something on the computer. Then she grabbed a file and headed toward the double doors. I watched closely as she punched in the code that opened the doors: 3326. She walked through the doors, leaving the whole front station empty. This was the perfect chance to see Sam.

I tiptoed up to the keypad, punched in the code, and slipped through the doors without anyone noticing. The only question was, what room was Sam in? I started walking down the hallway. Outside of each door was a file with the patient's name on it. At the very end of the hall, I found the one labeled "Goodwin, Sam." I took a deep breath and started to open the door when I heard someone come up behind me.

"Excuse me. You're not supposed to be back here!"

I turned around to see the same nurse I'd seen at the nurse's station just a few minutes ago. Her name tag said her name was Rosslyn Wiley. My heart started thumping wildly in my chest. I tried to speak, but no words would come out. The nurse's expression softened a bit.

"I didn't mean to scare you, sweetie. Do you have a family member in the ICU?"

I shook my head. "No."

"Do you know Sam?"

That's when the floodgates opened, and tears started streaming down my face. "Yes, he's my boyfriend. There was an explosion, and he was trying to help, but he ended up getting hurt. I just really need to see him. I need to know he's going to be okay."

Her lips became a straight line, and she shook her head. "Well, I'm afraid he's in really bad shape, and he's not supposed to have any visitors. Only immediate family. Are you the girl who was in the explosion with him?"

I was still crying, which made my words come out sort of choppy. "Yes. And I'm the one who made him go back in the building, so if something happens to him, I'm not sure I can forgive myself. I just need to see him for a minute. I'll be quiet. I promise."

The nurse pulled a package of tissues out of the pocket of her scrubs and handed me one. The she looked at me with eyes that were kind and sympathetic. "I could lose my job for what I'm about to do, you know that?"

"You mean I can …"

She nodded. "Hurry up before I change my mind."

Seeing Sam hooked up to so many tubes and machines was almost more than I could take. I felt like he was in this place because of me, and the guilt was overwhelming. I sat in the chair beside his bed and listened to the steady beat of his heart on the monitor, which was the only proof he was alive. He looked so pale, and when I took his hand, it was as cold as ice. I cleared my throat before I spoke.

"Hey, Sam. It's me, Rachel. I just wanted to tell you that I am so sorry for everything. I'm the one who should be lying in the bed, not you. And if I could change places, I'd do it in a heartbeat. I know I've made a lot of stupid mistakes, and I'm not very good at telling people how I feel, but you've changed me, and I can never thank you enough for that. Because of you, I know it's enough just to be myself. I also want you to know that I believe you. I believe everything you told me, and I want to help you help my dad. My mom says she's going to rehab, and I really believe her this time. If anything good came out of this, maybe I'll get my mother back. I don't want to get my hopes up too much, but it's something, right? I just need you to wake up." I bent down and kissed him on the cheek. "I love you, Sam."

For a few beautiful minutes, it seemed like it was just me and him. But then all of his machines started beeping like crazy, and his heart monitor went flat. A whole swarm of doctors and nurses ran in, including the nurse who let me in to see him. She put her hand on my shoulder and led me out of the room.

"You need to leave now, but don't worry. Your boyfriend is in good hands."

My throat tightened up, and it was hard for me to breathe. "Do you think he's going to be okay?"

She shrugged. "Nobody knows that but the man upstairs, and he's not talking. I do know one thing, though. Sam is a fighter. Now I want you to take care of yourself. Go up to your room and get some rest, okay? I'll let you know if there are any changes with Sam."

I nodded and headed toward the elevator. I turned the corner just as Mrs. Goodwin came out of nowhere and almost ran into me. She looked surprised to see me.

"Rachel, what are you doing here?"

I swallowed hard, realizing how thirsty I was. "I just needed to see Sam."

She narrowed her eyes. "Don't you think you've done enough damage? If it weren't for you, he wouldn't have been at

Burger Shack when the explosion happened. You made it out with a bump on the head, and we don't even know if Sam will make it. I could lose my only son. Do you have any idea how that feels?" She didn't wait for an answer before she continued her tirade. "I want you to leave Sam alone. You're no good for him."

I didn't know what to say, and even if I did, I didn't have the strength to form the words. So I just turned around and walked back to my room, trying to fight back the tears that were coming.

CHAPTER

19

When I returned to my room, Mom and Michelle were waiting for me, along with a woman I vaguely remembered as my grandmother. I hadn't seen her in years, but she still looked the same with a few extra wrinkles and salt-and-pepper hair that she wore to her shoulders. My mom crossed her arms over her chest.

"Rachel, where have you been? You're not supposed to be wandering around the hospital. Your nurse didn't even know where you were, and we were worried sick. Everyone in the hospital is probably looking for you."

I didn't have the strength to answer her. Instead, I ran into her arms bawling like a baby.

"You went to see Sam, didn't you?"

I nodded. "Uh-huh. And his heart stopped beating. They had to come in and revive him. Then I ran into his mom, and she blames me. I don't really blame her because I blame myself too. She didn't like me before, but now she can't stand me."

My mother didn't judge me or say, "I told you so." She just held me for a while until my sobs slowed down.

"Did you notice who came to see you?"

I tried my best to force a smile. "Hi, Grandma."

"Hi, Rachel," she said in her familiar, kind voice. "I hear you were quite the hero, bringing three people to safety after the explosion."

I shrugged. "I guess. I don't really feel like a hero, though. Sam did most of the saving."

"Well, you're one in my book. And I guess were going to be spending a lot of time together."

Mom nodded. "I'll be leaving in a little while for the treatment facility. So, I want you girls to be on your best behavior for your grandma. We probably won't be able to talk for a while. It's part of the treatment process. But I know this will be worth it in the end. It's a new beginning for all of us."

Michelle put her arms around her. "I'm proud of you, Mom. I know you can do this."

She took a deep breath. "I'm not going to lie. I'm scared to death. I've been numbing myself since your dad died, and now I have to let those feelings come out. It's not going to be easy, but the two of you are worth it." She looked at Grandma and smiled. "And I couldn't do it without you, Mom."

"We're all on your side. We want you to get better," Grandma said. "So don't worry about us. We'll be fine."

"I know you will," Mom said. "I mean, Rachel has been the head of the household for a long time now. She's a smart girl with a good head on her shoulders. I'm proud of both of my girls."

We all hugged before she turned to me with a serious expression on her face. "Oh, Rachel, I meant to tell you an investigator with the police department stopped by while you were gone. I suppose he wants to know about the explosion at Burger Shack."

"Well, there isn't much to tell," I said. "The building was old, so it was probably something electrical."

Mom nodded. "Well, I am just so glad that you're okay. I really hate to leave, but I need to finish packing. I signed the papers so that Grandma can be your legal guardian while I'm gone, and I will be in touch as soon as I can. As much as I hate being away from you, I know that this is what's best for all of us."

"Don't worry about us," I reassured her. "We'll be fine." She smiled. "I know you will."

And with those words, my mother walked out the door.

And I let out a big sigh of relief.

CHAPTER

20

I guess I should have been happy when it was time to go home, but all I could think about was the fact that I was going home while Sam was still in a coma. His nurse, Rosslyn, came in to tell me that he was stable for now. She'd promised to let me know if there was any change in his condition. Somehow, that didn't give me very much comfort. I needed to see for myself, but the thought of running into his mom made me feel nauseated. I started to pack my things when I was interrupted by a knock on my hospital door. I assumed it was my grandma there to pick me up.

"Come in."

Instead of my grandmother, Jessica Sinclair appeared in the doorway.

"Hi, Rachel."

My mouth formed a giant O. She was the last person I expected to see.

"Can we talk for a minute?"

I nodded. "I guess."

She slowly stepped into the room. "I just wanted to come by and see how you're doing, and I also wanted to apologize for being such a jerk to you. The truth is, I've always admired you. You work really hard at school and get straight As while keeping your job at Burger Shack and helping out with your sister. I only acted that way toward you because I was jealous, I guess—especially when Sam showed interest in you. I think I've had a crush on him since junior high. But I'm over that now. Why would I want to be with someone who doesn't like me back anyway?" She paused, thinking carefully about her words before she continued. "When everything went down at Burger Shack, it put things in perspective. Life is too short to spend it being angry, jealous, and bitter. So, I want you to know I'm really sorry for the way I acted. I don't expect you to just forgive me right away or for us to be best friends, but I am sorry."

I stood there in stunned silence. I never thought I would hear Jessica apologize, and I had no idea how to respond. But I didn't have the strength to argue with her anymore. I had other, much more important things on my mind. "Okay. I accept your apology."

Jessica looked surprised. "Really?"

"Sure. I mean, we don't have to be best friends or anything. We can just agree to disagree. I'm tired of fighting all the time."

She nodded in agreement. "Me too. Okay, well I guess I will let you get back to packing. I bet you can't wait to get out of here."

I sighed. "That's an understatement. I just wish Sam was doing as well as I am."

"How is he?" Jessica asked as she walked toward the door.

"Still the same," I told her. "In a coma."

"Well, if anyone can come out of this better than ever, it's Sam. Keep me updated, okay?"

"Sure."

"All right. Well, I guess I'll see you at school."

With those words, Jessica slipped through the door, leaving me speechless.

When there was a second knock at the door, I was sure it was my grandmother, but I was wrong again. Two police officers entered my room, one short and round with almost no hair and one tall and lanky with a thick head of jet back hair. They both smiled.

"Hello," said the taller one. "Are you Rachel Walters?" I nodded. "That's me."

"I'm officer Peter Dodson, and this is my partner, Craig Harris. Were just here to ask a few questions about the explosion that happened at Burger Shack the other night. Is now a good time?"

I swallowed a big lump in my throat. It would never be a good time to relive that awful night. But I knew they would probably just come back, and I wanted to get it over with as soon as possible. "Okay. What would you like to know?" Officer Harris pulled a notepad from his pocket. "You were finishing your shift at Burger Shack before the explosion happened, correct?"

"Yes, but I wasn't in the building when it happened. I was in the parking lot."

He nodded and jotted something down on his notepad. "Another witness said that before you walked out to the parking lot, there was an altercation between yourself and another girl from your school, Jessica Sinclair?"

I wondered what Jessica had to do with all of this, but I answered. "Yes."

"And can you tell me a little about that argument?" The officer's words were kind but stern.

I still didn't understand why this was important, but I wanted to help any way I could. "We both liked the same boy, and Jessica has been a bully since we met. She was trying to get to me, and I let her. I lost my cool."

"And was this boy you fought over the same one who was injured after the explosion? Mr. Sam Goodwin?"

The sound of his name sent shivers down my spine. "Yes."

"And he is still in the ICU?"

"Yes," I answered, sadly.

Officer Harris's face turned more serious. "Do you think it's possible that Jessica Sinclair might have had something to do with that explosion?"

I felt my whole body turn numb. "No, I don't think she would do something like that. I mean, she's been a bully in the past, but I don't think she would go to that extreme. Besides, she was just here. She apologized and sounded really sincere."

Officer Dodson took a deep breath. "Sometimes, a person will apologize out of guilt when they know they've done something really wrong and want to take it back. We're just here to try to put together the pieces of the puzzle—to figure out what might have happened. It's our job to turn over every rock and look at every possibility. There is an investigation going on that might tell us more about the cause of the explosion, but for now, we just have the word of the witnesses."

All of a sudden, my throat went dry. I replayed everything in my head, from the time I came to take Jessica's order until I handed her Kristen and ran back into the building. Jessica and her friends were giggling to themselves at the table, which in itself wasn't alarming. They acted like that all the time. But why would she come back to Burger Shack? I was so caught up in the moment, I didn't even take the time to ask myself that question. Had she been waiting nearby watching to see if her plan had worked? Would she really stoop to that level? I took a big gulp of my water.

Officer Harris put a kind hand on my shoulder. "Is there anything you noticed that day, before or after the explosion, that looked suspicious to you?"

I shook my head. "No."

"Is there anyone you know who might want to harm Burger Shack or someone in the building?"

"No … I don't think so."

"Well, if you do think of anything else that might be important, just give us a call," Officer Dodson said as he pulled a card out of his pocket and handed it to me. "And thanks for your time today. I hope your friend gets better soon."

And with that, they walked out of the room, leaving me alone again with a million thoughts racing through my head.

CHAPTER

21

"I bet you're ready to get out of here," Grandma said as she helped me pack up the rest of my things. "It's been a long few days for you—and for all of us."

I nodded. "Yes, it really has. It feels like it's been a year."

"Well, you'll be home before you know it." She smiled her sweet smile, and I knew everything would be all right. My grandma always had a calming effect on everyone she came in contact with, and I felt lucky to have her on my side.

Just then, a little girl came running into my room. I recognized her almost immediately as Kristen from the explosion. "There she is, Mommy. That's the girl who saved both of us!"

A woman followed her into my hospital room. I recognized her as Kristen's mom. Of course, she now had all of the color back in her cheeks, and she wore a huge smile. "Sweetie, you can't just run into people's hospital rooms like that. It looks like she's getting ready to leave, just like us."

"I just wanted to thank her," Kristen said with an adorable little pout on her face.

"It's okay," I assured her. "Kristen and I are old pals, right?"

The little girl beamed, and it made me feel good all over.

"It's good to see both of you together and happy," I said.

"Well, we really can't thank you enough," Kristen's mom said. "Did they ever find out what happened? I mean, what the cause of the explosion was?"

I shook my head. "They're working on it. he police are doing an investigation, so hopefully they will get some answers soon."

"Well, that's good," she said. "It was so sudden, and I just can't imagine anyone doing something like that on purpose."

I nodded in agreement. "Yeah, it was really something."

"And what about the other guy who pulled Mommy out of the fire?" Kristen asked. "Is he okay?"

I took a deep breath. For one split second, I had forgotten about Sam in the ICU. "He's going to be in the hospital for a while," I told her. "He was really hurt when a light fixture fell on him. But the doctors are doing everything they can for him."

The little girl nodded sadly. "Well, I made each of you a picture. Maybe this will make him feel better."

She pulled two pictures out of her pocket and handed them to me. They both had rainbows and flowers all over them, and I smiled. "I'm sure this is just what Sam needs to feel better," I told her. "Thank you."

She smiled a huge smile. "You're welcome."

When we walked through the door to my apartment that afternoon, everything felt different somehow. Everything was in the same place, but it just didn't feel like home anymore. I quickly tossed my belongings in my room and paced around a bit, but I couldn't seem to relax. How could I when Sam was still in the ICU?

I thought about my dad's spirit walking around and not being able to talk to anyone, at least not anyone who could hear him. That was enough to make me feel on edge. Then I started thinking about who would try to hurt anyone on purpose. Were the two detectives right about Jessica? Would she really stoop to something so extreme? I tried to convince myself that couldn't be true, but it did make sense.

And finally, I thought about the fact that I didn't have a job, at least not until they rebuilt Burger Shack, and that would probably be a while. With the unpaid bills waiting for me and an impending eviction, I really needed that paycheck. But more than that, I just needed to know that Sam was going to be okay.

Pinned to my bulletin board was a picture of Sam and me the night of Michelle's play. He looked so handsome in his suit and tie, with that big cheesy grin on his face that I couldn't get enough of. We both looked so happy, and I would have done anything to go back to that time. Now he was hooked up to a bunch of tubes and wires, and I couldn't shake the feeling that it was my fault.

I vaguely heard a knock at the front door, but I didn't think anything of it until Michelle came bouncing into our room.

"Someone's here to see you."

"I don't want to talk to anyone."

"I think you'll change your mind when you see who it is."

I sighed as I stood up and walked out to the living room, and my heart almost stopped when I saw Mrs. Goodwin standing there.

"Hi, Rachel," she said. Her voice seemed softer somehow. "I bet you're surprised to see me."

"That's an understatement."

She took a deep breath before she continued. "Sam is awake. He's been asking for you."

I let out a huge sigh of relief. "Thanks for letting me know, but you made it pretty clear you don't want me to see him."

She nodded. "I did say that, but I was wrong. I am here to apologize for the way I've treated you. I thought I was protecting Sam, but deep down, I really do want my son to be happy, and you seem to make him happy. Besides, he threatened to disown me if I didn't let the two of you see each other. So, who am I to stand in the way of young love?"

I stood there in shocked silence. "Does this mean what I think it means?"

She nodded. "You'll need to make the visit short. He does need his rest. He's not out of the woods yet, but the doctors are optimistic he'll have a full recovery."

Those words were music to my ears.

CHAPTER

22

When I walked into Sam's hospital room, I was filled with so many emotions I couldn't even describe. Seeing him sitting up in his hospital bed with a big grin across his face made me feel so happy. I wanted to run right to him and wrap my arms around him, but I stood there frozen. He still had a lot of tubes and wires, and I didn't want to hurt him.

Sam just rolled his eyes and patted the spot next to him on his hospital bed. "What are you waiting for?"

I practically ran to him and tackled him with a hug. I could feel the tears trailing down my face.

"I thought I'd never see you again."

"It's going to take a lot more than some stupid light fixture to get me down." Then he looked up at his mom and his nurse who were standing in the doorway. "Can I have a few minutes alone with Rachel?"

They nodded and walked out to the hallway, closing the door behind them. Sam and I just held each other for a while, no words were needed.

When he finally spoke, I couldn't believe my ears. "Are you okay?"

"Am I okay? You were the one in a coma. I just had a bump on the head and some smoke inhalation. I was really worried about you."

He reached over to wipe away my tears. "Well, I'm going to be just fine. I have so much to tell you, and I don't even know where to start. Did you know that my heart stopped for a few minutes? I was technically dead."

I felt a fresh batch of tears trail down my cheek. "I know. I was freaking out. I wasn't sure if you were going to make it."

Sam gently tucked my hair behind my ear. "Well, when that happened, I saw heaven."

I almost choked on the lump on my throat. "You did?"

"Yes, and it was beautiful. There were so many colors, and I felt this sort of peace—something like I've never felt before. And I saw some of my family members who have been gone for years. I honestly never wanted to leave. I wanted to stay there forever, but there was one thing that made me want to come back."

I took a deep breath. "What was that?"

"You. I heard everything you said when you came in to see me."

I felt my heart start to pound. "Everything?"

He nodded. "Yes. You told me that you believed me about my ability to talk to people who had died. And you told me you wanted to help your dad reach the other side. There was one other thing you told me. Do you remember what that was?"

It took a few moments before I could answer. "I told you that I love you."

"Did you mean it?"

I nodded. "Of course I did."

He beamed. "I love you too, Rachel. I love you so much. And that's what made me want to come back. That's what kept me here. I want you to know that. Maybe at first I wanted to get to know you because your dad told me to. But It's because of him that I met the smartest, funniest most awesome girl in the world. And for that, I will be forever grateful."

I melted into him. "I'm sorry I didn't believe you at first. It was so much to take in. But I did mean every word I said."

He squeezed me tight. "I know you did. Now there's just one more thing. In order for your dad to find peace and go where he's supposed to go, he needs you to do something."

"What's that?" I asked, curious.

"He needs you to forgive the guy who shot him."

I shook my head. "I can't do that."

Sam sighed. "I thought you might say that. I know it's not going to be easy, but I'll be with you every step of the way. As soon as I get out of here, I'll go with you to visit him in prison. It might make it easier if you hear his side of the story."

"I don't want to hear his side!" I snapped. "He killed my dad. I don't think I can ever forgive him for that."

Sam ran his fingers through my hair, trying to calm me. It worked because I could feel my heart rate go down a bit. "You're stronger than you think you are, Rachel. Do this for your dad."

I hesitated for a long time before I nodded. "Okay, I'll do it."

CHAPTER

23

"I changed my mind. I can't do this," I said to Sam as we walked toward Folsom Prison. Even though it was a beautiful day outside, the gray concrete walls made it feel so cold. I felt sick to my stomach. I just wanted to leave. I wanted to be anywhere but there.

Sam just squeezed my hand, giving me the strength I needed. "You're stronger than you think. You can do this for your dad."

I took a deep breath and nodded. We continued toward the building where visitors signed in.

"I used the online process to request a visitation, so we are already preapproved," Sam told me. "All we have to do is check in. Our names should already be added to the list." After we checked in, a very large man with black hair and a beard led us to a room where the inmates met with visitors. It all happened like a whirlwind. All of a sudden, the man who shot my dad was sitting right in front of me. There was a security guard stationed in the corner, but there was nothing separating us.

My throat felt tight, and I felt like I was going to pass out. I wanted to be anywhere but there, and I wondered how Sam talked me into this. Harry looked different than I had imagined him all of these years. He had dark hair that almost reached his shoulders, but it seemed well-kept. He seemed young, thirty at the most, but his eyes looked like those of an old man. They were hazel and kind of sad, like he had a story to tell.

He sat down in a chair across from us and looked at us. I could tell he was curious about why we were there to visit him. I wondered if anyone had come to visit him during the ten years he had been in this place, but I pushed those thoughts aside. Why should I care if he'd had visitors or not? This was the man who had ruined my life. It was because of him that my dad would never get to watch me go to college or walk me down the aisle. He had stolen that from me, and I wasn't sure I would be able to forgive him for that.

Harry cleared his throat. "Do I know you?"

I shook my head, gathering the strength to speak. "You don't know me personally. My name is Rachel. This is Sam." He looked confused. "Are you here to do some sort of school report on the prison system? Because if you are, I'm not interested."

"I'm not here on a school assignment," I assured him. "This is much more personal."

All of a sudden, Harry's eyes flashed with recognition. "You're Fred's daughter, aren't you?"

Anger washed over my body, and I'm sure I shot him some daggers. How dare he speak my father's name like he was a friend or even an acquaintance? He had no right. And how did he even know he had a daughter?

"How did you know that?" I mumbled, trying my best not to show how shocked I was. I wasn't going to give him the pleasure of getting a rise out of me. He didn't deserve it.

He took a deep breath and looked me right in the eyes. "I read the articles in the paper, so I knew Fred had two daughters. I've always wanted to meet you, so I could tell you how sorry I am for what happened to your dad."

Right then and there was when I lost it. I stood up with rage flowing through my body.

"You're sorry? Sorry isn't going to bring my dad back, is it? You took him from us when you shot him! He only went in to the store that day to get me an Icee. He saw you and your friend robbing the place, and being the good guy he was, he tried to stop you. But the gun fired, and my life was changed forever because of something you did. I'm supposed to be here to forgive you, but I don't know if that's possible right now." I looked over at Sam. "I want to go home."

Sam put his hand on my shoulder. "Maybe you should listen to what he has to say."

"Maybe I don't want to hear it," I said.

Harry looked at me with compassion and pity. "I know sorry doesn't bring your dad back. I live with that every day of my life. It honestly doesn't matter if you forgive me because I will never forgive myself for ending his life. Believe me, that was never my intention. I was about your age when it happened, and I was at the lowest point in my life. My mom had died of a drug overdose just a few months before. My dad was never a part of my life, so that left me in charge of my ten-year-old brother, Benny.

"He was all I had, and I wanted to do right by him, but I was just a kid myself. We were put in a foster home, which was more like the house of horrors. The guy beat us every day and made us do some pretty disgusting things just to get food. Benny had always been a happy kid, but now he would barely talk to anyone. Then he started hurting himself, and one night he even swallowed some pills to try and end his life.

"I knew we had to get out of there, so one night I packed our bags and we left. I didn't know where we were going, but anywhere was better than where we were. I wanted to get a job so I could take care of Benny, but no one would hire me because I was only seventeen and had a history of getting into fights. I spent every last penny I had on a beat-up used car that broke down all the time, and that's where we slept. We had nothing. I didn't know when we would eat next, and I knew if we stayed in one place for long, they would take Benny away. The thought of losing him made me desperate.

"I didn't care about myself, but Benny had so much potential. He was smart and very artistic. Some of his drawings had even won awards. I didn't want his light to go out. I had to do something. We even resorted to begging on the streets for cash. We had this whole sob story rehearsed, which really wasn't far from the truth. And that's when we met Ronny.

"He saw us begging for money, and he told me there was a better way. He offered to let us stay for free in this condo he rented out and even stocked it with all of our favorite foods. We thought we'd hit the jackpot. Benny started doing better; he almost seemed like his old self. But there was a catch. Ronny wanted me to help him.

"First, he had me delivering packages. I was a I kid, and I did that without questioning it. After all, it seemed like a small price to pay to have a roof over my head, all the food we wanted to eat, and my brother back. But one night, he told me he needed more. If I wanted to continue staying in his condo, I had to help him. And if I didn't help him, he would hurt Benny. He handed me the gun but promised we weren't going to hurt anyone. He said it wasn't even loaded; it was just there to scare the cashier at the store so he would give us the money. I didn't like it, but I agreed to do it because I didn't feel like I had a choice. And I swear to you that I didn't know the gun was loaded. I was shocked when it went off.

"I never meant to hurt your dad. I know that doesn't make it okay, and I know that won't bring him back, but I will spend the rest of my life wishing I could take it back. That's my reality, and it's something I will live with the rest of my life. So, while I know sorry doesn't make it better, it's all I have. I don't expect you to forgive me, but I am glad you came so I could tell you that."

I stood there frozen for a long time, taking in everything that Harry had said to me. He was nothing like I'd expected, and even though I didn't want to admit it, we were more alike than I ever could have imagined. His relationship with his little brother was a lot like my relationship with Michelle. And although we didn't lose our mother to a drug overdose, we came close a few times. I thought about what I would have done if I had been in the same situation. He didn't have the support of a grandmother like Michelle and I had. All of a sudden, the anger I had was replaced with something else. I'm not sure if it was pity or forgiveness, but I felt a sort of peace I hadn't felt for a very long time.

"Thanks for sharing that with me," I said, slowly meeting Harry's gaze. Tears slowly trickled down his cheek, and I quickly wiped away my own tears with the back of my hand. "I didn't know what to expect when I came here today. I didn't even want to come, but now I'm glad I did. I guess I always thought of you as some sort of monster, but you're a lot like me."

He looked surprised. "I am?"

I nodded. "After my dad died, nothing was the same. I had to take charge at a very young age. I had to step up and be a mother to my sister, pay the bills, and take care of my drug-addict mom. It wasn't easy, but I am lucky that I have a lot of support."

I reached over and squeezed Sam's hand. He had been such a huge support, and I couldn't imagine my life without him. I noticed he was tearing up a little bit too, and that made me love him even more.

I cleared my throat before I continued. "I wish that you'd had that kind of support back then. If you had, maybe you wouldn't have been so desperate. Maybe you wouldn't have gone into the store that day, and maybe my dad would still be here."

Harry took a deep breath. "I would give anything if I could make that a reality. I really am sorry."

I smiled and reached out to take his hand. "I know, and I forgive you."

He looked shocked, and tears continued to trail down his cheek. "Thank you."

Sam smiled and placed his hand on my shoulder. "I think it's time to go now, Rachel."

I knew exactly what he meant. My dad was ready to move on. That was exciting and terrifying at the same time. Part of me wanted to keep him here with me forever, but I knew I had to let him go. I stood up to say my goodbyes, but I had one more question for Harry.

"Do you know what happened to Benny?"

He shrugged. "After I was arrested, they put him in another foster home. I haven't heard from him since. I like to think he found a family who loves him and he's doing great with a successful art career. That's all that keeps me going in here."

"I hope so too," I said as I took Sam's hand. We walked out of that room with a whole new perspective about everything.

CHAPTER

24

Later that day, Sam and I sat by our spot by the river, hand in hand, looking out at the water. It was a little overcast that day, but it was still one of the most relaxing places to be. The sound of the water gurgling was a peaceful melody, and I knew this was the right place to say goodbye to my dad.

"I was proud of you today," Sam said, breaking the silence. "It took a lot of courage to go to the prison and listen to what Harry had to say."

I nodded. "Thanks. I didn't think I could do it at first, but now I'm glad I did. I feel kind of sorry for Harry. It doesn't seem fair that he's stuck in that jail cell while that other guy Ronny is running free. I think he's the one who should be punished."

Sam squeezed my hand. "I agree. I guess life isn't always fair, is it?"

"No, it's not," I said almost in a whisper.

Sam scooted in closer to me, wrapping his arm around me. He always knew how to make me feel loved and safe. I wondered why on earth I wasted so much time trying to push him away.

It all seemed so pointless now. I didn't want to waste one more second I could be with him. I couldn't imagine ever being with someone else now. He was my future, my forever.

Sam smiled, seeming to read my mind. "We really have been through a lot together in these last few months, haven't we?"

"Yes, we have," I said.

"And you know I love you more than anything, right?"

"I know."

"I want to be with you forever."

I felt chills spread through my body—in a good way. "I want that too." It was then that I noticed Sam had carved our names with a heart around them in a tree by the edge of the river. Somehow, seeing our names carved there seemed so permanent, and I had a feeling that nothing could come between us now.

He smiled his big, dopey grin, but it didn't annoy me anymore. "Your dad wants us both to know he approves, and he's happy your mom is finally getting the help she needs. He's here to say goodbye before he crosses over."

When I looked out at the water, there was a ray of light that wasn't there before, and I felt a gust of warm air. I swear I could see my dad waving at me. Then I heard him whisper, "I'll always be with you." And just like that, he was gone. The ray of light disappeared. I wished for a sign that he reached his destination and that he was happy and finally at peace. And all of a sudden, it started pouring down rain. That's when I started laughing hysterically.

Sam looked at me with a confused expression. "What's so funny?"

"My dad loved the rain," I told him. "We used to put on our rain gear and play in the rain for hours."

"Maybe this is his way of letting you know he's all right," he said, and I agreed.

We both looked up at the sky and smiled. It started raining even harder. Then we kissed, and although we had kissed many times before, this time was different. I can't explain what was so different about it, but it was. We kissed in the rain for the longest time, until we were both drenched. Neither one of us made any sort of effort to move; we were exactly where we wanted to be. There were no rules, no boundaries; it was just us. It wasn't until I started to shiver that Sam sat up and reached out to take my hand.

"Let's go change out of these wet clothes."

Sam's house was eerily quiet as we walked through the door. I scanned the house, expecting to see his parents or one of the housekeepers. Sam seemed to read my mind.

"My parents are away for a business meeting, and they won't be back until Tuesday. And Rosalee is visiting her family for the weekend, so it's just us."

I swallowed a huge lump in my throat. For some reason, my heart was pounding out of my chest. I followed Sam up to his room, where he handed me one of his T-shirts to change into while he put our clothes in the dryer. It was light blue, comfortably worn, and smelled just like Sam's aftershave. I thought to myself that I never wanted to take it off. I lay back on Sam's bed, and I realized how tired I was. It had been an emotionally exhausting day.

"Our clothes should be dry soon," Sam told me as he came in and sat on the edge of the bed. He was wearing a white T-shirt with a pair of teal boxers. He had never looked better.

I quickly pulled him down beside me and rested my head on his chest. I realized that if I ever wondered what love felt like, this was it.

"Thanks for being there for me today," I whispered. "I really couldn't have done it without you."

Sam smiled, gently running his fingers through my hair. "I'd do anything for you. I hope you know I mean that."

"I do."

I reached over and kissed him with all of the passion I had in me, knowing that there was no way I had the willpower to stop. I reached for the bottom of his white T-shirt and pulled it over his head, admiring his bare chest more than I cared to admit. He was all muscles, and that made him even sexier. I kissed him on the stomach, on the chest, and worked my way back to his lips. Then I tugged at the waistband of his boxers, wanting to see more of him. To my disappointment, he stopped kissing me and pulled away.

"Maybe we should stop."

My heart dropped. "Why?"

"Because if we go any further, I don't know if I can stop."

I smiled. "Good, maybe I don't want you to. I do want you to know I've never done this before."

Sam looked relieved. "Me neither."

I was surprised and relieved. I'd always pictured Sam with a dozen different girls before me. But the thought of being his first sent chills up my spine. I wanted him more than I had ever wanted anything. I looked him in the eyes, wanting him to know how sincere I was.

"Let's be each other's first ... and last."

"Are you sure? Because I don't want you to feel pressured to do anything you're not ready for. We can wait. I'm not going anywhere. I promise."

I put my finger over his lips. "I don't want to wait. I want you now."

With that, Sam slid his T-shirt over my head, gently kissing me all over my body. I had always been self-conscious, but not with Sam. I knew he loved all of my imperfections.

"I love you, Rachel," he whispered.

I'm not sure if there is a word for what happened next, but if there was, it would be perfection.

CHAPTER

When the Sacramento County Fair came to town, Sam and I took Michelle and her friend Amy. We had offered to take Grandma, but she opted for a quiet afternoon at home. It was hard for her to walk a long distance anyway, and she was too stubborn to rent an electric scooter.

With only a few short weeks in the school year and graduation right around the corner, life was busy, to say the least. I'd applied to a few nearby colleges, although I still didn't know exactly what I wanted to do. I decided I could take my general education courses while I figured it out. I honestly didn't know how I would afford college anyway, even with all of the scholarships I had applied for. Grandma had offered to help, but I didn't want to depend on her too much. She had already done enough for us.

Our mom was scheduled to finish her rehab program and be home in time for my graduation. I'd only had a few short conversations with her, but it seemed like she was in a good place. We were all ready to have her home.

THE PROMISE

They had started rebuilding Burger Shack; it would be under new management when it reopened in the fall. They discovered that the explosion was caused by a gas leak in the kitchen and someone's discarded cigarette. It was nothing more than a freak accident. When I think about all of the ways that explosion had changed my life, I knew everything happened for a reason. Sam and I were closer than ever now, and his mom was more accepting of our relationship, which made things way easier in so many ways.

As soon as we waked through the gates of the fair, Michelle headed straight for the food court, trying to decide what she was going to eat.

"I think I want one of those giant turkey legs," she said, pointing to a man who was eating one while he walked around. "And a deep-fried Twinkie for dessert."

I giggled. "Are you always thinking about your stomach?"

"Only when there's so much good food around."

"Well, why don't you and Amy go on some rides first?" I suggested. "We can meet back here in a few hours to eat."

"Okay!" Both girls cheered as they headed for the carnival rides.

Sam reached over to take my hand. "Alone at last."

"What do you want to do first?" I asked.

Sam shrugged. "Let's look at the exhibits in that building. There's always some cool stuff in there."

We walked around looking at different exhibits that were done by 4-H and Scout groups. It was amazing how much time and effort some of the kids put into their projects, and it made me wish I'd encouraged Michelle to do something like that. Then I realized I was still thinking more as her mother than her sister, and I was trying to stop that mindset. After all, Mom would be home soon, and I would be starting my new venture in life, whatever that might be.

We entered the building where people were selling things, which was fun because we got to try out some really cool stuff. We even tried out a state-of-the-art massage chair. Sure, people would try to get us to buy their products, but we would politely tell them no. Then we passed a booth where there was a man who claimed to be a psychic medium. It said on the sign his name was Magic Mike, and for only twenty-five dollars, he could communicate with your loved ones who had passed on or predict your future. He was in deep conversation with a little old lady who wore her gray hair in a bun. She looked at him with sad eyes.

"I can see your husband," he told her. "His name was Carl, right?"

The little old lady looked disappointed. "No, his name wasn't Carl."

Sam shook his head. "That guy is so full of it. I can't believe he would take her money. He has no idea what he's talking about."

"Was his name Kevin?" Magic Mike continued.

"No"

"James?"

She shook her head and frowned. "No, and I don't think you could communicate with my husband even if he were here. I want my money back."

Magic Mike rolled his eyes and pointed to the sign behind him. "Sorry, lady. No refunds."

The little old lady frowned. "But you weren't able to do what I paid you to do."

"Well, if you want me to try to contact another family member, maybe I will have better luck."

"My husband was all I had," the lady whispered.

All of a sudden, Sam had had enough. He stormed over to Magic Mike. "Who in the hell do you think you are?"

Magic Mike glared at him. "I'm Magic Mike, psychic medium."

"No you're not," Sam snapped back. "And you'd better give this woman her money back or else."

"Or else what?" Magic Mike demanded, his eyes growing colder. "It clearly states on my sign that there are no refunds. If I do it for her, then I would have to do it for everyone. Mind your own business, kid."

Sam got in his face. "You really are a piece of work, but you're no psychic medium."

Magic Mike stood up, and I realized how tall he was. I suddenly felt sick. I thought there was going to be a brawl right then and there.

"Who are you to tell me what I am?" He shouted. Sam ignored him. He knelt down to the old lady's level and put his hand on her shoulder.

"Linda, I want you to know your husband, Jack, is here, and he wants to tell you goodbye. He says he's sorry about the necklace."

Her mouth dropped open, and she pulled a diamond-shaped pendant out from under her shirt. "He accidentally dropped it in the garbage disposal, but I took it to the jeweler and they were able to fix it. How did you know?"

Sam glared at Magic Mike. "Because unlike some people, I really do have the ability to communicate with dead people." Then he turned his attention back to the little old lady. "Jack said to tell you to read the note he left in the nightstand, and he says he will always love you."

She smiled. "I found the letter, but it's too soon to open it."

"He says he knew you would say that," Sam told her. "But he told me to tell you it's time to let go but not to worry. You will see him again before you know it."

"Okay, I guess you're right," she agreed. "Sixty years of marriage is a long time. I guess I've taken this really hard." She looked from Sam to me, and her smile brightened. "We were young and in love once, just like the two of you. His mother didn't like me for some reason, can you believe it? But we didn't let that stop us for one second. We had two great kids who now have kids of their own. Now I would give anything just to hear him snore. Promise you won't take that for granted. I can tell the two of you have something special."

Sam and I looked at each other and smiled. "We won't," we said in unison.

Sam cleared his throat. "Okay, it's time now. Jack is ready to cross over. He just wants to tell you one more thing."

"What's that?"

"He wants you to fly out to see the kids and grandkids. He wants you to mend the falling out you had with your son, and he says not to let your fear of flying get in the way." Linda smiled a bright smile. "I've been thinking of planning a trip back East. Who knows, I might just decide to stay. When Jack was sick, his doctors were here, but nothing is keeping me here anymore." Then she looked up with tears in her eyes. "Goodbye, my love. See you soon."

I felt a warm gust of air, which I guessed was Jack leaving this world for another one, and Linda seemed at peace. "Thank you, young man. I don't believe I got your name?"

"Sam, and this is Rachel."

She patted him on the shoulder as she walked away. "I hope you two have a wonderful life together, like Jack and I did. I just have one word of advice."

"What's that?" I asked.

"Compromise." She walked into the crowd of people without another word.

I reached out for Sam's hand, trying to avoid eye contact with Magic Mike. "Come on, Sam. Let's go."

As we started to walk away, Magic Mike grabbed Sam's arm. A look of rage came over his face.

"That wasn't cool to call me out in front of all of these people. But I want to know how you knew all of that? You actually had me believing it too. What's your secret?"

Sam pulled his arm out of his grip. "This wasn't some sort of parlor trick. I don't take money from little old ladies just to lie to them. I'm the real deal."

An envious smile came over Magic Mike's face, and he picked up a business card from the table and handed it to Sam. "If that's true, then maybe we could go on the road together. We could make a fortune, you know. A gift like that shouldn't be wasted. I can be the one to help you make the most of it."

"I'm not wasting my gift," Sam said, tearing up the business card. "I just don't use it to take advantage of people." He reached for my hand. "Come on, Rachel. Let's go."

"You'll regret this!" Magic Mike called out, but we ignored him as we walked away.

∞

"That was amazing!" I said to Sam as we walked through the art exhibits. "The way you were with that old lady. I think you really helped her move on."

Sam nodded in agreement. "It helped that she was so open to the idea. If the person is closed off, it doesn't work as well."

I was just curious about one thing. "I thought you told me you wanted to keep it between us—your gift, the ability to talk to dead people. So how come you were so public about it today? I'm not sure if you noticed, but you had a big crowd around you, and that Magic Mike guy wasn't too happy you trumped him on the whole psychic medium thing."

Sam nodded. "I do usually like to keep my abilities quiet, but there are times I know it can really help someone, like Linda. So, I make a choice that the benefits outweigh the risk. And I have to admit, I enjoyed giving Magic Mike a little taste of his own medicine. He deserved it. But I do want you to keep this between us, Rachel. Most people don't understand."

"Your secret's safe with me," I promised.

"There were times I just wanted it to go away," he admitted. "I felt like I was so different from everyone else, and I guess it's just human nature to want to fit in. But helping Linda today makes it all worth it."

"Well, I wouldn't change a thing about you," I told him, meaning it.

Just then, we passed a youth art exhibit done by an afterschool program, and I stopped to admire some of the drawings done by middle school kids. They were mostly of the sunset, some over the river, which reminded me of the time I'd spent there with Sam.

"Do you like them?" a young man asked. He was sitting behind a table at the exhibit, and he looked vaguely familiar, like I had seen him before, but I couldn't place him.

"Yes, these are really good," I said. "Especially for middle school kids."

He nodded in agreement. "These are all kids in my afterschool art class. Some of them have really been through a lot, but art is such an amazing way for them to express themselves. It helped me when I was having a rough time, so I wanted to give back. Anyway, if you want to know more about the programs we offer, you can check out our website."

He reached for a business card on the table and handed it to me. I glanced at it, thinking it sounded like a good program for Michelle. But when I read the name on the card, I couldn't believe it. *Benjamin Davis.*

"Benny," I whispered. "It couldn't be."

He looked confused. "No one has called me Benny since … for a really long time. Do I know you?"

I shook my head. "This might sound like a strange question, but do you have a brother named Harry?"

He cringed and took a few steps backward. "I did once, but he did something really awful, so I haven't talked to him for years."

I could feel tears well up in my eyes. "I saw your brother, and I know that he misses you. It would mean the world to him if you would visit."

His eyes suddenly grew a shade colder. "I guess I don't understand. How did you know my brother?"

A lump began to form in my throat. "He shot my dad." Benny's mouth hung open in shock. "And you're telling me to go visit him?"

"I know it's crazy, but when I heard his story, I forgave him. He made a mistake because he was desperate, and he wanted to protect you. If you would just listen to his side, I promise you won't regret it."

Benny met my gaze. Tears were forming in his eyes. "Maybe you could forgive him, but I don't know if I can. He promised he would never leave me. I would have rather been on the streets with him than in some of the foster homes they put me in. I idolized my big brother."

Sam put his arm around me before he looked at Benny and said, "He idolized you too. He knew you would do something in art, and he would be so proud of you."

"You think so?" Benny asked, hopefully.

Sam nodded. "I know so."

We spent the rest of our night at the fair going on rides, eating junk food, and playing carnival games. It had been such an amazing day I never wanted it to end. Michelle and Amy had a great time too. We all got a giant turkey leg, but Michelle was the only one to finish hers. Then we finished it off with a deep-fried Twinkie for each of us which we topped in our own unique way. We ended the night on the Ferris wheel, where Sam and I kissed under the stars. It was one of those perfect days I will never forget, and if I knew how much my life was about to change, I would have stayed there forever.

CHAPTER

26

Math finals were especially challenging. It had never been my strongest subject anyway, and it didn't help that I had been nauseated for most of the day. I couldn't eat breakfast and was only able to eat a little bit at lunchtime. I didn't have time to be sick with finals and graduation, but there I was, running to the bathroom in the middle of my calculus final, where I threw up the salad I'd had for lunch. I went to the sink to splash some water on my face when Jessica walked in, looking a little pale herself.

"Are you okay?"

I nodded. "It must be something I ate."

All of a sudden, she turned white as a ghost and ran into the stall where I heard her throwing up too. *Great.* I thought to myself. There was some sort of stomach bug going around, and it had perfect timing. When she came out, she splashed some water on her face and looked at herself in the mirror.

"Some stomach bug, huh?" I said, grabbing another paper towel and handing it to her.

"I wish," she told me, looking down at the ground. "I'm afraid it's something much more serious."

"More serious? Like what?"

Her expression changed to something more like panic, and my heart jumped in my chest. "I'm pregnant, Rachel."

"What?"

"You heard me right. I'm pregnant, and Todd wants nothing to do with the baby, so I have no idea what I want to do next. I can't handle a baby on my own. I haven't told my mom yet; she's going to kill me."

I had no idea what to say next, so we both sat in silence for a while.

"So maybe you don't have a stomach bug," she continued. "If there's any chance you could be pregnant, you should take a test. The sooner you know, the better, right?"

I froze, staring at my reflection in the mirror. There was no way I could be pregnant. Sam and I were only together that one time, and the timing wasn't right in my cycle for anything like that to happen, was it? The more I thought about it, the faster my heart drummed in my chest. I knew that anything was possible, and I was a little late ... or a lot late. I hadn't been keeping track lately. Suddenly, I bolted out of the ladies' room, out of the school, and to the Walgreens down the street.

I must have been speeding to Sam's house that afternoon, rehearsing in my mind what I would tell him. I was still in shock myself, so I had no idea how I would tell him we were expecting a child. Sure, we had talked about having kids in the future, but there were so many things we wanted to do before then. How were his parents going to react? We had already had a rocky start, so I was sure this would add fuel to their fire. And my mom would be coming home next week. This was just what she needed. I was sure it would send her spiraling out of control again, and all over a choice I made.

As I pulled up to Sam's house, I noticed two police cars parked in the driveway, and I started to panic. I turned off the engine, threw open the car door, and practically flew to the front door, where I pounded on the doorbell until Mrs. Goodwin opened the door. I could tell she had been crying; mascara was smeared all over her face.

"Rachel, it's so good to see you," she said, throwing her arms around me. "I've been trying to call you."

"What's wrong?" I asked, glancing at the police officer who was sitting at the dining room table talking to Mr. Goodwin.

"Sam never came home last night," she told me. "He told us he was going for a drive, but he never came home. The police found his car down the street in a ditch by the side of the road. It looked a little banged up, but there was no trace of him. You haven't heard from him, have you?"

I shook my head, realizing he had never showed up for world history finals. "I didn't see him at school today. I was hoping to talk to him."

She took a deep breath. "It's just not like him to disappear like this. Something's wrong. I can feel it."

She wrapped me in a hug, and I hugged her back. "I'm sure it's just a misunderstanding," I told her. "He'll come home soon." *He has to.*

I told the officer everything I knew. The last time I'd seen Sam was that night at the fair, and we had talked briefly on the phone the next day. He had given no sign that anything was wrong, so where was he now when I needed him the most?

It wasn't like him to disappear without calling. I should have known something was wrong when he didn't show up at school, but I was so focused on doing well on my finals, I didn't think anything of it.

After I had given my statement to the police officer, Mrs. Goodwin and I promised each other we would call if we heard anything from Sam, and then I jumped in my car and sped off on a wild-goose chase, hoping to find him.

As I checked off every place Sam could be with no luck, I started to realize that something was very wrong. He would have called me by now to check in; he wouldn't want me to worry like this. Where could he be? I'd checked his friend Mark's house, our favorite frozen yogurt place, and, of course, our spot by the river, which sat eerily empty. I traced my finger over the heart Sam had carved with our names on it on a tree.

"Where are you, Sam?" I whispered with tears rolling down my cheek. "I really need you."

But the only answer was the gurgling of the river.

CHAPTER

27

The next few weeks were a whirlwind of emotions. Despite a huge search for Sam, he never showed up. With each passing day, the chances of finding him grew slim. The coverage of Sam's disappearance was still on the news, although it had died down a bit. I still had a lot of morning sickness, which I blamed on the flu. I hadn't told grandma yet; it just didn't feel right to tell anyone before Sam. I spent most of my time in bed, only coming out to eat or use the bathroom, which I had been doing a lot of lately.

"Are you going to sleep all day?" I heard Grandma say as she knocked on my bedroom door one Sunday morning.

"I'm still not feeling well," I mumbled.

"Moping around isn't going to bring Sam back, so I'll tell you what you're going to do," she said in her best Grandma voice. "You are going to get out of bed and take a shower because nobody wants to smell you. Brush your teeth and hair, put on a little makeup, and come to church with me."

"What?" I had only been to church a handful of times in my life, mostly when I was really young. After Dad died, Mom just didn't want to go.

"We leave in an hour, so you'd better hurry up," Grandma said finally. "I made pancakes for breakfast."

I knew when Grandma had her heart set on something, she wasn't going to let it go, so I dragged myself out of bed and hopped in the shower. The water felt good, and I actually started to come to life for the first time in days. I slipped on a nice blouse and a pair of slacks. I wasn't sure what the dress code was at church, so I went with the nicest thing I had to wear. The only other option was the dress I had picked out for senior ball, which I would probably never have the chance to wear. I had planned on going with Sam, and there was no way I would go without him.

A breakfast of pancakes and bacon was waiting for me when I came to the kitchen. Although I tried to be polite and eat, I was still feeling a little nauseated.

"This is so good!" Michelle chirped, smacking her lips together as she ate.

"Would you stop doing that?" I snapped.

"Doing what?"

"That!" I said, gesturing toward the food that was falling out of her mouth.

She pushed her plate away. "I don't know what's gotten into you lately. It's not my fault Sam disappeared."

"You two be nice to each other," Grandma said. "We've all been through a lot lately, and that isn't anyone's fault. I think church will be good for everyone, so let's finish breakfast so we can go."

Church was different from how I had pictured it. Everyone was warm and friendly, coming up to greet us as soon as we'd arrived. The praise band opened with "Amazing Grace," and then Grandma introduced us to her church friends. She seemed proud to show off her granddaughters, and I wondered if she would still be proud if she knew the secret I was keeping.

Pastor Dan was in his mid-fifties, but he had a youthful look about him. He was wearing jeans and a blue button-up shirt, which made me feel better about my clothing choice. The church had a casual feel, and when he got up to speak, I felt like he was talking to me instead of at me.

"Sometimes life's circumstances can really bring you down," he began. "We can have a bad day, a bad month, or a bad year, and when we do, many of us wonder where God is. Why hasn't he been there lately? When will he finally listen? Well, he is there, people. He hears you. And even in those hard times, he has a plan for you. You may not understand what his plan is, and he might not even answer your prayers the way you think he should. But in those darkest moments, there is a light."

Those words repeated in my head over and over. *In those darkest moments, there is a light.* I wondered what that light might be because right about then, I couldn't see it. But then pastor Dan introduced a guest speaker who changed everything. Her name was Angelica, and she was a young woman, maybe a few years older than me. She had curly dark hair and a warm smile, which made me wonder what she could possibly have to share with us. And then she spoke, and the whole room became silent in a matter of seconds.

"A few years ago, when I was just shy of eighteen, I was going through a rough patch," she began. "The challenges of finishing high school are overwhelming for anyone, but especially when you come from an abusive home. My father stayed out late drinking every night. When he came home, it was only long enough to beat my mom, my sister, or myself. I put on a good front. To the rest of the world, I looked like I had it all together. In fact, I was a straight A student. But I was dying inside.

"When finals came around, I was looking for something to stay awake so I could study. And then I met Jack. He was captain of the football team, and he was charming. He said he had something that would help me focus so I could ace the finals. The only catch was I had to be his girlfriend. It seemed like a fair trade to me at the time. He was handsome, smart, everything a girl could want.

"I started taking the pills, and they worked. I felt invincible, until I started to need more and more of them. I depended on Jack to get the pills for me, and I was willing to do anything to get them. Jack promised he would be there for me no matter what … until I found out I was pregnant, and then everything changed. All of a sudden, he wanted nothing to do with me or the baby growing inside me. He told me I'd better get an abortion, or he would beat me until I lost the baby. I had never been so afraid or so alone. I felt like I couldn't share this with my parents, and my friends wouldn't understand. They all thought we were the perfect couple.

"But one day I saw a flyer on the school bulletin board that changed everything. It was for the Options for Life Pregnancy Center. They give prenatal care and counseling to those who can't afford it, which is a good thing because I had no insurance and no money. At first, I was dead set on getting an abortion. It seemed like the right thing to do. There was no way I could support a child.

"But as soon as I had that first ultrasound, everything changed. There was this little life inside me, and I wanted to give him or her a chance. I still wasn't sure if adoption or parenting was right for me, but I was determined to give this little person the best life possible. As my pregnancy progressed and I started to feel the baby moving inside me, I knew I wanted to find a way to raise my child. It wouldn't be easy, but I knew through experience that life was rarely easy. With some help from the staff at Options for Life, I was able to find a job at a doctor's office and get my own apartment.

"It was June 20 when I gave birth to my amazing son, Chance. I named him Chance because I took a chance and decided to raise him, which was the best decision I've ever made. And since then, I have made peace with my parents, and I also met a wonderful man who loves Chance just like he's his own son, and we got married six months ago. My life isn't what I had imagined five years ago, but it's so much better. If I had given up and not seen things through, I wouldn't have the life I have today. Now, would you all like to meet Chance?"

Everyone cheered as a man who I assumed was her husband came out holding an adorable blonde-haired, blue-eyed little boy who was waving at everyone. I swear there wasn't a dry eye in the house.

After church, there was a barbeque where everyone could stay and socialize. I really wanted to go home and crawl into my bed, but I plastered a fake smile on my face because Grandma seemed so happy and I hated to disappoint her. We sat at the same table with Angelica and her family, and I couldn't stop staring at her as she played with her son, who was all smiles. I put my hand to my stomach, wondering if the baby I was carrying was a boy or a girl and if he or she would look like Sam, me, or a combination of the two of us.

"He's really cute," I complimented.

Angelica beamed. "Thanks. He's what keeps me going, you know? But it hasn't always been easy. These little stinkers don't come with instruction manuals, and I hadn't been around kids much before I had him, so it was a big adjustment. But I think we've got a good rhythm going now. Don't we Chance?"

Chance giggled in agreement, as he smeared mac and cheese all over his shirt.

"I think it's time to go change him," Angelica said with a sigh. "If you'll excuse us."

She scooped up Chance and walked toward the bathroom, while I sat there picking at my food with a million thoughts going through my head. But the one main thought was, *What would I do next?*

CHAPTER

28

"Can I help you?" The receptionist at Options for Life greeted me with a smile. She had kind eyes, and I knew right away I was at the right place. I had taken a flyer from church, and I figured this would be my best option since I didn't have any insurance or a way to pay for this.

"I spoke to someone who said I could come in for an ultrasound," I said in a whisper. I wasn't sure why I was whispering, but it wasn't something I wanted to blurt out.

She smiled. "Yes, absolutely. Just fill out this form, and someone will be with you shortly."

She handed me a clipboard, and I sat in the waiting area and filled it out. There were only a couple of other people there, and one sat with her face in her hands, crying. I couldn't see her face, but I would recognize her anywhere. It was Jessica. I walked over and sat down beside her. She looked up at me with a tear-streaked face; her smeared mascara made her look a little like a racoon.

"Rachel? What are you doing here?"

"It turns out you were right. I'm pregnant too." Her eyes widened. "You are?"

I nodded. "And I have no idea what I'm going to do."

"Me either," she said quietly. "I still haven't told anyone. Todd told me to get an abortion, but I don't know if I can do that. But I also know there's no way I can raise a baby on my own."

I nodded in agreement. "If Sam were here, I honestly think we could make this work, but he's not. And at this point, chances are he might not ever come back."

Jessica looked at me with a mixture of sadness and pity. "It's crazy how he vanished into thin air like that. You guys were the perfect couple, and if anyone could have made this work, it would be you and Sam. I hope you know how truly sorry I am for trying to come between you, and I'm sorry you're going through this all alone."

"Yeah, it kind of sucks," I said. "My mom gets out of rehab soon, and this isn't exactly the kind of news she's going to want to hear. It could make her regress."

"Or maybe she will support you," Jessica pointed out. "You don't know until you try, right?"

"Right, and neither do you," I said. "You should at least try to tell your mom."

"Okay," she said with a sigh. "But until then, I say we make a pact—to be there for each other and give each other support, no matter what choice we make."

I smiled. "That sounds like a good plan."

Just then, a receptionist poked her head out from behind the door. "Rachel Walters?"

"That's me." I stood up and walked toward the door. "Good luck, Jessica."

"Thanks." She beamed, and for the first time, I saw Jessica Sinclair in a different light. She was someone I might actually call my friend.

༄

A spunky, dark-haired lady with kind brown eyes greeted me in the exam room. I was already undressed from the waist down and feeling more than a little self-conscious, so it helped that she was so upbeat.

"My name is Regina, and I'll be doing your ultrasound today," she told me. "So, it says here you're not sure when your last menstrual period was?"

I shook my head. "No, I've been so busy with finals, and my boyfriend disappeared, so I don't remember. Is that a problem?"

"Not at all," she assured me. "It is helpful, but we can measure the baby and find out how far along you are. Now, are you ready for this?"

"As ready as I'll ever be."

Within seconds, I was looking at the little cashew that was growing inside me with a tiny beating heart that made a swoosh sound. It was music to my ears. I just wished Sam could be there to see it too.

"Everything looks great," Regina said with a smile. "It looks like you're almost eight weeks along."

"That's about what I figured," I whispered.

"I want you to know we are here to support you and your unborn baby whether you decide to parent or if you are interested in adoption. Do you have a strong family support system?"

I shook my head. "Well, the baby's dad is missing. I'm sure you probably heard of Sam Goodwin?"

She nodded. "I saw the story on the news. I'm so sorry."

I shrugged. "That's life."

"So, have you told anyone else?" she asked, curious.

"No. My mom is coming home from rehab soon, and I haven't had the heart to tell my grandma."

"No matter what decision you make, you are going to need their support," she told me. "Sometimes it's like ripping off a bandage. There might be a little shock at first, but in the end, it will be worth it."

I nodded, feeling only slightly more confident than I did when I got there. I still had no idea what I was going to do.

CHAPTER

29

The night my mom came home I made her favorite comfort food—fried chicken with mashed potatoes and corn. I was both excited and nervous to have her home again. I wanted so badly for this to be a fresh start, but she had let me and Michelle down more times than I could count. I wanted to believe things would be different this time, but part of me didn't want to get my hopes up just to have them crushed again.

When she walked into the apartment, there was a sign Michelle made that said, "Welcome home, Mom," and the smell of fried chicken lingered in the air. She smiled and hugged us both.

"It's so good to be home."

"It's good to have you home," I told her.

"I am so sorry about Sam, sweetie. He was such a nice kid."

I felt a little pang of sadness that she talked about Sam in the past tense. I didn't want to believe he was gone forever.

"They are still looking for him," I reminded her.

"Of course they are, and I hope they find him soon. I want you to know that things are going to be different this time, Rachel," she promised. "I want to be the parent I never was to the two of you. I hope you believe me."

"I really want to," I said.

"We do believe you, Mom," Michelle corrected. "And we're proud of you."

"Thank you," Mom said with tears in her eyes. "Now, if you don't mind, I am going to unpack my things and take a shower. I haven't had a decent shower in months. I'll be out in a little while for dinner if that's okay."

"That's fine," I assured her. "And, Mom?"

"Yes, Rachel?"

"Welcome home."

⁂

"This is so good, Rachel," Mom complimented a little while later as we all sat around the table. "I don't know what you put in this fried chicken, but it is probably the best I've ever had."

"She's right, Rachel," Michelle agreed. "It's the bomb dot com."

I laughed at Michelle's choice of words. It felt good to have everyone together again, but Grandma just sat quietly, stirring her mashed potatoes. I wondered what was going through her mind.

"Thanks for the compliments, but I really couldn't have done this without Grandma's expertise," I said. "It was her mom's secret recipe."

Mom smiled at Grandma. "Thank you so much for holding down the fort, Mom."

"It was no problem at all," Grandma assured her. "I enjoyed the time with the girls. It was good to be needed again." All of a sudden, she buried her face in her hands and started to cry.

Mom walked over and gave her a hug. "What's the matter, Mom?" she asked, starting to tear up a bit herself.

"Now that your home, I guess you all don't need me anymore," she said through her tears.

"We still need you, Grandma," Michelle and I said in unison as we got up to give her a hug.

"I know," she said. "But it won't be the same. You guys need to reconnect as a family. If I stick around, I will only be in the way."

"You would never be in the way," I said. "We need you now more than ever."

"You guys will be just fine without me," she said with a flick of her hand. "Besides, this apartment is way too small for the four of us."

"And one more on the way," I whispered.

"What was that, Rachel?" Mom asked.

"I'm pregnant," I blurted out as I scooped a huge pile of mashed potatoes onto my plate.

Everyone stared with their mouths gaping open like I had just told them the world was going to explode. Of course, it was my sister who broke the silence. After the shock wore off, she started dancing around the table.

"I'm gonna be an auntie! I'm gonna be an auntie!" she cheered.

"Hold your horses, squirt," I told her. "I haven't exactly decided what I am going to do yet, but there's no way I'm prepared to raise a baby, especially since Sam's not around." Michelle's cheers quickly turned into a frown. "But I can help.

I'll babysit all the time. I even know how to change a diaper. I took that babysitting class at the Red Cross, remember?"

"There's a lot more to it," I assured her. "Kids cost a lot of money. I don't have a job, and who is going to hire me now? I feel like this baby would be better off if I find a nice family to adopt him or her."

Michelle's frown turned into tears. "But what if Sam comes back? Won't he be mad you just gave away his kid?"

"The chances of that happening are slim at this point."

I looked at Mom and Grandma for some sort of support. Mom just took a deep breath before speaking. "I can't believe this happened in the few months I was away. I mean, I thought we had the talk. I thought you were prepared for this sort of thing. You were my responsible one, Rachel."

"Well, you weren't here, and things happen," I told her. "I personally wouldn't give up one second I had with Sam. He was my rock through a lot of hard times. He was the love of my life. But now I have to face reality without him. This baby will be here in seven months, whether I am ready or not. So, I have to make the right decision for him or her."

Mom and Grandma both looked at each other and nodded.

"We will be here to support you no matter what," Grandma said. "I will find a place that is close so I can be there for you, at least until the baby is born."

"Thank you, Grandma."

"That's what family is for."

Michelle got up, quickly rinsed her plate, and put it in the dishwasher. "I still don't think you should just give away your baby like it's nothing, but I guess my opinion doesn't matter."

With that, she stomped off to our room and slammed the door behind her, and I knew this would be the hardest decision I've ever had to make.

CHAPTER

30

Over the next several months, I slowly started to come out of my funk. Jessica and I went to the senior ball together. It might have just been an excuse to wear the dresses we both had, but it did lift our spirits. It is amazing how immature most of the high school seniors were, and the drama was something I will never forget. I laughed so hard my side hurt.

Never in a million years would I guess that Jessica Sinclair and I would become friends, let alone best friends. But we understood each other in a way no one else did. We even walked with each other at graduation, where I graduated with honors. It was a happy day, but it did make me think of Sam. He would have been so proud of me.

Mom got a job working at a department store, which she loved. She always came home telling me funny stories about the customers and the behind-the-scenes gossip she heard in the break room. It seemed like she was really on track, and I was proud of her. It was good to have my mom back.

Just like she'd promised, Grandma found a great senior apartment complex nearby, one with some great amenities like meals and laundry service. She said she never used those because she wanted to cook for herself and do her own laundry as long as possible. "The day I can't take care of myself is the day you should put me out of my misery," she said with a smirk. Grandma always had the best sense of humor, and I was so happy to have her in my life.

Michelle and I hadn't talked much since I told her I was considering giving my baby up for adoption. She continued to sulk and give me the silent treatment. But I knew I had to do the best thing for this baby, and the more I looked into it, the more confident I was in that decision. Options for Life helped me contact a wonderful adoption agency called Bright Beginnings, and I started interviewing families who might possibly raise my baby. None of those families seemed right. They were too old or too young, too strict or too lenient, too quiet or too loud. I was starting to think maybe I was being just a little bit too picky and I would never find the right family at this rate. Then I met the Swansons, and everything changed.

We met at Starbucks, and I knew right away this was the right family. They were a good-looking couple and had been married for more than ten years. They were both teachers. Amy taught first grade, and Dan was a middle school English teacher. This meant that they would have lots of time during school breaks to spend with the baby. They planned on spending the summer together as a family and traveling, which was something I always dreamed of when I was younger. And when Amy shared her story about their journey to start a family, it gave me the chills. She tucked a strand of her strawberry-blonde hair behind her ear and took a deep breath before she began.

"When we got married ten years ago, we wanted to start a family right away. We were already almost thirty, but we thought it would just happen naturally. When it didn't, we both thought something must be wrong with us. We had four miscarriages over four years. Three of them happened early on, and the last baby made it to term and lived for forty-six beautiful minutes.

"She had a terminal brain condition called anencephaly, which we found out about halfway through the pregnancy during an ultrasound. If she even survived birth, she wouldn't live very long. She would never walk, talk, or breathe on her own. A lot of people thought we were crazy when we decided to carry her to term, but we wanted to hold on to our daughter as long as we could. Feeling her move inside me is something I will never forget. When Olivia was born, they wrapped her in a little pink blanket with a little pink hat, and our family all came and held her and said goodbye. It was so special. She was so beautiful and perfect. Then we made the hardest decision we've ever made to donate her organs so another child could live. We even had the pleasure of meeting the little boy who has our daughter's heart." With that, Amy started to cry, and Dan squeezed her hand and took over.

"It took us a long time after Olivia before we were ready to try again, but we finally decided to try IVF. We spent our entire savings, and after three failed attempts, we vowed to never put ourselves through that nightmare again. So, we opted for adoption. We contacted Bright Beginnings and went through all of the classes and home visits. We felt like we were being looked at through a microscope, but we told ourselves it would be worth it when we were holding our child. Well, twice we were connected with birth mothers who choose us to be their baby's parents. We went to ultrasounds. We had a nursery ready. We even picked out names. And then, twice, they backed out at the last minute. They decided they wanted to keep the baby. I'm just telling you this so you know we are at the end of our rope. After four failed pregnancies, three failed cycles of IVF, and two failed adoptions, we both agree this is our last shot at being parents. So, if there is any doubt in your mind about giving your baby up for adoption, please just tell us now because we can't take any more heartache."

I took a deep breath and wiped a tear from my eye before I was able to speak. "My dad died almost eleven years ago in a convenience store shooting. I've been taking care of my drug-dependent mother and my little sister ever since then. I've spent most of my life taking care of other people, and it has been a lot to deal with. There were times I wanted to give up. Then I met Sam, and everything changed. He was my person, my best friend, and the one I wanted to be with forever. But now he's gone, and the police say there is a very slim chance he's still alive. My mom just got out of rehab, and there is no way I can raise this baby on my own. I have thought about this long and hard. I want the best life for this baby, and I know without a doubt that's not with me. It's with you. I want you to raise this baby, and I promise I won't change my mind."

Dan reached over and took Amy's hand, and they both hugged and cried. Then we all joined in a group hug, and they must have thanked me about a hundred times. I patted my stomach, knowing I had made the right decision for my child. A feeling of relief washed over me, but it was mixed with a little sadness. In a few short months, I would be saying goodbye to a little part of Sam forever.

THE PROMISE

Later that day, I sat at our spot by the river, watching the water rush by, deep in my thoughts. Even though Sam wasn't with me, that spot still brought me so much peace. I traced my finger over Sam's name on our tree, thinking of all the wonderful memories we had here.

"I found a great family for our baby," I said through my tears.

"I want you to know that I've thought long and hard about this, and I know it's the best thing. If you were here, things might be different. We might have found a way to raise this baby together, but there's no way I can do this on my own. I want to give our baby the best chance at a life I never had, and I know this is the best way to do that. I know the Swansons will take really good care of him or her. They have wanted a family for a really long time now, and I want to do this for them, but I am still feeling so lost. I wish you were here, Sam."

My tears started falling faster, and I sat down on a sandy spot by the bank of the river. "If you're somewhere out there, can you just give me a sign that I am doing the right thing?" And right after I said those words, the rain started to fall, and I looked up at the sky and smiled.

CHAPTER

31

"I found a family to adopt the baby," I told Michelle as we sat at Baskin-Robbins sharing a banana split. I knew the best way to get through to Michelle was through her stomach, and the silent treatment was driving me crazy.

"Are they nice?" she asked, carefully scooping a bite onto her spoon.

"They're the best," I assured her. "They have wanted to be parents for a really long time now. I know this is all hard for you to understand, but I know it's the best thing for everyone. Mom just got out of rehab, and I want to go to college. There is no way I can raise this baby on my own. And maybe someday, when he or she is a little older, the baby might get curious and come find us. I know the Swansons do plan on telling the baby he or she is adopted, and they would be open to that sort of thing. So maybe we will get to be a part of this child's life, at least in some capacity."

"It's not the same," Michelle said. "We'll miss her first steps and her first words. I wanted her first words to be *Auntie Michelle*."

I laughed. "Aren't first words usually something simple, like mama or dada?"

"Well, this kid is going to be a genius. She is part Sam, and he was pretty awesome."

I stirred my ice cream, deep in thought. "Yeah, he was. So, how do you know it's a she?"

Michelle shrugged. "Just a hunch." We both ate our ice cream quietly for a few minutes before she continued. "If you think this is the right choice for you and the baby, then I guess I do too."

"Thanks. I really am going to need all the support I can get."

She nodded. "Sorry I've been such a jerk about the whole thing."

I picked up the cherry from the top of the banana split and popped it into my mouth. "You're forgiven. Love you, little sister."

"Love you too, big sister."

As the months went by, my belly grew and grew. Halfway through the pregnancy, I couldn't wear any of my nonmaternity clothes, and I couldn't imagine getting any bigger, even though I had several months to go. I asked the doctor if I was having twins, but he assured me there was only one baby in there.

The Swansons came with me to all of my appointments, and they loved listening to the baby's heartbeat. About halfway through the pregnancy is when they do a big ultrasound of the baby to check all of the vital organs. It's also when they can tell the gender of the baby. I had already decided I didn't want to know, but I was leaving it up to the Swansons since they might want to decorate the nursery in pink or blue.

"So, are you hoping for a boy or a girl?" I asked as we waited for the ultrasound technician to enter the room.

"We're just hoping for a healthy baby," Dan said matter-of-factly. "The gender doesn't really matter."

Amy laughed. "I think Dan has always dreamed of having a daughter. Someone to take to daddy-daughter dances and be his little princess. But as long as the baby is healthy, that's all we're hoping for."

"Well, this little one sure has a healthy kick," I said. "And a healthy appetite. I can't seem to get full. He or she seems to really crave chicken chow fun."

Amy giggled. "It will be interesting to see if the baby still likes that when he or she is old enough for solid foods." Then she looked at Dan and back at me with a more serious tone. "There is something Dan and I have been wanting to ask you."

"What's that?"

Amy cleared her throat. "We know the baby's father is missing without a trace, but what about his parents? Do they know about the baby?"

I paused, taking a deep breath. The truth was, the Goodwins didn't know about the baby, and I didn't plan on telling them. Seeing them was too painful. They reminded me too much of Sam, and I think they felt the same way about me. Besides, I didn't want anybody or anything trying to change my mind about giving the baby up for adoption. Maybe that was selfish of me, but it's how I felt. Of course, I didn't want to scare the Swansons away. They had already had enough heartbreak for a lifetime. So, in order to spare their feelings, I lied.

"Yes. Sam's parents know about the baby, and they are on board with my decision." I felt horrible as soon as I said those words, but it seemed to give the Swansons some peace, so I felt a little better about lying to them.

Just then, the ultrasound technician came in, a nice-looking woman with long, dark hair pulled into a ponytail.

"Are we ready to take a look at this baby?" she asked with a smile.

"Yes," we all chimed in.

The tech put some warm gel on my stomach and got started. Since I was required to have a full bladder, it was really uncomfortable when she pressed down with the Doppler, but in seconds, there was a beautiful image on the screen. The baby had gotten much bigger since the last scan and no longer looked like a little alien. It was a fully formed person, who seemed to be sucking his or her thumb. Dan put his arm around Amy, and they stared at the screen in awe.

After some time, the ultrasound technician looked up from the screen. "Would you like to know the baby's gender?" I shook my head. "There is no reason for me to know. But since they will be the ones raising this kid, I will leave it up to them."

Amy nodded. "Yes, we want to know."

The ultrasound technician smiled as she pulled a piece of paper and a pen out of the pocket of her scrubs and scribbled something down. Then she folded it and handed it to Amy, who carefully unfolded it and held it up for her and Dan to see. And they both smiled the biggest smile I had ever seen.

CHAPTER

32

Amy's mother threw a huge baby shower for the baby-to-be, which I was invited to because, of course, I was the one carrying the baby. It felt a little awkward at first, but it was kind of nice to meet the family that my baby would be a part of. There were a ton of aunts, uncles, and cousins. it was the kind of big, loving family I had always wanted. Amy's niece and nephew, Tommy and Ellie, were adorable as they ran around in the back yard laughing and playing.

"Why is your belly so big?" Ellie asked, examining my stomach.

"That's because there is a baby in there," I told her.

"Is it a boy baby or a girl baby?" she asked, curious.

I looked over at a box placed on a table with pink and blue balloons that said, "Boy or girl?"

"I don't know yet, but I think they are going to announce that after I leave."

Tommy giggled. "Why is it such a big secret?"

I shrugged. "I guess it's more fun that way."

They seemed satisfied with my answer and continued playing hide-and-seek. I watched as Dan played with them, and I could tell he would be an amazing father. Still, I wished Sam would have the chance to be a father, and I wondered what could have happened to him. Six months later, it was still as big of a mystery as it was the first day he disappeared.

"Rachel, would you mind coming over here for a minute?" Amy's mom, Maggie, called as she patted the seat beside her.

I went and sat down, feeling just a little bit nervous. "I want you to know we are all so excited to welcome this baby into our family," she said. "It really is a blessing, especially after everything Dan and Amy have been through to be parents."

I nodded. "They told me it has been a really long road." All of a sudden, her posture changed, and she straightened up a bit and became serious. She looked over at Amy, who was mingling with the party guests. "It's been hard to watch my daughter go through all of that, especially when we lost Olivia. It was just heartbreaking."

"I'm sure it was," I said, meaning it.

"I just want to make sure that you are absolutely sure about this because there is no turning back, and I couldn't take it if my daughter got her heart broken again. That has happened before—twice. The birth mothers changed their mind at the last minute."

"I know, and I don't plan on changing my mind. Maybe that has happened in the past, but that's not me. This is their baby. I'm just the delivery service," I assured her.

She seemed to relax a little and reached over to give me a hug. "Thank you."

"You're welcome."

The rest of the party was wonderful, and I knew I couldn't have picked a better family for this baby. So, I pushed aside my lingering feelings of doubt and plastered a gigantic fake smile on my face.

CHAPTER

33

When Burger Shack finally reopened, I went with Michelle, Mom, and Grandma for lunch. It felt strange to be there as a customer instead of an employee, but as I ran my hands over my now humongous stomach, I knew I was in no condition to work there even if I wanted to. My ankles were swollen, and I waddled everywhere I went.

Burger Shack was completely remodeled now, which took away some of the nostalgic appeal. But it still held many memories for me. A picture of Mr. Thompson was hung on the wall with a nice plaque that said, "Thank you for 30 years of service." After the fire, he decided to retire and move to Florida with his wife. This was long overdue since he had talked about it for years, but he would be missed, that was for sure. A few of the same employees were working there, but most were new. They all seemed so young even though they were only a year younger than me. Goes to show you how fast life can age you sometimes. We sat in a booth near the window, and Michelle quickly flipped through the menu before she decided what to order.

"I want the chili cheese fries and a chocolate shake!" That reminded me of the day Sam came to Burger Shack and ordered the exact same thing. I felt a pang of guilt that I had been so rude to him that day.

"I just want a salad," Grandma said, patting her stomach. "I've been dating again, so I need to watch my girly figure." I laughed, enjoying the moment with my family and feeling grateful they were in my life. I honestly didn't know what I would do without them. Mom and I both ordered a cheeseburger and an iced tea, knowing that Grandma would want to sample the cheeseburger. She always wanted what was on everyone else's plate. We never complained, though. Grandma wasn't getting any younger, and lately, she had been forgetting things more often. The other day, she asked where that nice young man I was dating was. I knew she was talking about Sam, and it was hard to have to tell her again that he was missing without a trace.

As we were eating, I started to feel kind of strange. It wasn't like the indigestion I had felt through most of the pregnancy. This was different. I stiffened up, holding on to my stomach.

"Are you okay, sweetie?" Mom asked.

I nodded. "I think so." But then another shooting pain hit, feeling like someone had punched me in the stomach. I also had the overwhelming urge to use the restroom. I stood up, and a big gush of water trickled down my legs and all over the floor. I knew what that meant, and it terrified me. "I think my water just broke."

My mom looked at the puddle I was standing in. "We should get you to the hospital."

"But this can't be happening!" I panicked. "The baby isn't due for another three weeks."

"It looks like this kid has other plans," Mom said calmly. "I'm sure everything will be just fine."

"No, it won't!" I snapped. "The Swansons are on their babymoon in Tahoe, and I don't even have my hospital bags packed."

My mom put her arm around me. "We will call the Swansons, and I'm sure they will make it back for the big event. And I promise after we get you checked in, I will go home and gather your things. We have plenty of time. Labor can go on for hours, especially for the first. I was in labor for three days with you, but Michelle just popped out, ready to eat right away."

I laughed, and a calmness washed over my body. I looked over at my sister, who was eating her chili cheese fries, oblivious to what was going on. "Hey, squirt. It's time," I told her.

"Time for what?"

"For me to have the baby."

She looked up at me with a serious expression. "Are you sure?"

"Yes!" Mom, Grandma, and I all said at the same time.

"Okay, okay. But can I bring my fries?"

"I guess, but hurry up."

Michelle put her fries in a to-go container, and we headed off to the hospital.

By the time we got to the hospital, I was doubled over in pain and convinced something must be wrong. Normal labor couldn't possibly hurt this much. But I forgot about the pain for a minute when I saw Jessica being wheeled in by a nurse at the same time. From the looks of it, she was deep in labor.

"You too?" I joked, but she didn't think it was funny. As a matter of fact, she started crying.

I reached over to pat her back in an effort to comfort her. "Don't cry. It's going to be all right."

"That's easy for you to say!" she snapped. "You have this wonderful couple to adopt your kid. I have nobody. My mom kicked me out. I don't even have a place to live. I've been staying with friends, but that's only temporary. I wish I had planned ahead like you. I wish I had a family picked out for my kid, but I wasn't sure what to do. What I do know is that I am not ready for this. I can't raise this baby, but I want her to have a happy life—the kind of life I always wanted."

I didn't know what to say, so I just held my friend for a while until her sobs started to quiet down. Then the nurse wheeled her into the exam room, and we went to check in at the reception desk.

"Can I help you?" a kind blonde woman who looked to be in her thirties said, greeting us.

"Yes, my daughter is in labor," my mother answered for me, as if I didn't have a voice of my own. "Her water broke about twenty minutes ago."

The woman nodded and typed something in the computer. "Okay, go ahead and go to exam room 2. Get undressed from the waist down, and a doctor will be in shortly."

I did as I was told, and it seemed to take forever for someone to come and check on me. Finally, a doctor came in, with kind eyes and a big smile. I was glad that it was a female doctor, for obvious reasons.

"Hi, I'm Dr. Owens," she said cheerfully. "So, I hear your membranes ruptured?"

"My what?"

"That's another way to say your water broke."

"Oh, yes. I mean I think so. Unless I peed on myself."

"Well, let's check you out and see what's going on."

I laid back on the exam table while she examined me, but then a surprised look came over her face.

"Have you been experiencing any contractions?"

I had absolutely no idea what contractions felt like because this was my first time ever being pregnant, but I had started to feel some sort of cramps the day before.

"I don't know. I mean, I started feeling kind of funny yesterday, but I didn't think anything of it, especially since the baby isn't due for another three weeks. I'm giving him or her up for adoption, and the adoptive parents are out of town, so I sure hope the baby can hold on until they get here. I mean, the plan was for them to be in the room when I have the baby and to hold him or her right away."

I saw the look of concern on the doctor's face, and my heart stopped for a minute.

"Is everything all right, Doctor?"

She paused for a moment. "Everything is fine, but you're already at ten centimeters. This kid is ready to come out."

My mouth formed a giant O. "But that wasn't in the plan. I thought I had more time."

"Well, sometimes things don't go as planned," she said in a comforting voice. "The good news is, one of our new luxury delivery rooms is available. Your family can be with you for support, if you want."

I looked over at the picture of a waterfall that hung on the wall in shock. "I'm not ready."

The doctor smiled. "Don't worry. You will be."

The next few hours were a blur of pushing, screaming, and the most intense pain I had ever felt in my life. I wondered how women all over the world could go through this every day and why people kept having kids if it hurt so much.

Mom and Grandma were there, feeding me ice chips as I pushed and holding my hand, whispering words of encouragement. Michelle sat over to the side, covering her eyes. We had given her the option of sitting in the waiting room, but she insisted on being in the room. Mom had called the Swansons, and they were on their way. Unfortunately, road conditions and traffic were horrible, so it would take them a while to get to the hospital. I tried to keep the baby in as long as possible, but my body had other ideas, and with on final push, I heard the most beautiful cry I had ever heard.

"She's here!" the doctor announced. "And she has a good set of lungs on her."

The doctor and her team took the baby to the other side of the room to weigh her and clean her up.

"You did good," Mom said as she bent down and kissed me on the forehead.

"Yes, you did," Grandma agreed. "And she's beautiful"

"Look at my niece." Michelle beamed. "Can I hold her?"

Mom looked over at the baby and smiled. "No, sweetie.

I don't think that's such a good idea. She's not ours to keep, remember?"

Michelle nodded sadly, and Mom put her arm around her. "I think it's time to go out to the waiting room so they can get Rachel cleaned up and comfortable. The Swansons will be here soon, and I'm sure they will want time with their new daughter. She looked at me and smiled as they walked out of the room, and then they looked over at the baby one more time before they closed the door.

I couldn't help but stare at the baby as they cleaned her up and put a beanie on her head. She had stopped crying now, but her eyes were wide open. She seemed to be watching everything the nurse did. I wondered if she thought she was her mother. Finally, they wrapped her in a blanket like a little pink burrito. Dr. Owens walked over to me. I wondered how on earth she was still so calm after she delivered a baby. I guessed she was used to that sort of thing.

"The baby looks great," she announced. "Just a little over six pounds, and twenty inches long."

I wasn't sure if that was average or not, but the doctor seemed pleased, so I was too.

"I just want to ask you one thing," the doctor continued. "Would you like to hold her until the adoptive parents get here? We usually do some skin-on-skin bonding right after birth, but I know this is a different situation. We can take her to the nursery if that's too difficult."

I looked over at the tiny squirming baby who now had her normal pink color. She seemed to be looking around for something, or someone. I knew that this might be my only chance to hold her before she started her new life with the Swansons.

"Yes," I answered. "I want to hold her."

The baby was placed in my arms, and before I knew it, everyone left, and it was just the two of us. I looked down at her and realized I had never seen anything so beautiful. She had big, round eyes; a cute button nose; and pink lips that seemed to smile. I removed her beanie and almost started to cry when I saw that she had tuffs of wavy dark blonde hair, just like Sam's. And then, I started to talk to her.

"Hi, I'm your mother. I mean, you grew inside me, but don't get used to looking at my face because you have a mom and dad who are on their way. I picked them for you, so they are extra special. I promise they are going to take such good care of you. They have wanted a baby like you for a long, long time, so they are really excited to meet you. I know it's confusing, but I just can't take care of you the way I should right now. Your daddy isn't around, and I can't do this by myself. You deserve better. You deserve a family where you have a mom and a dad and lots of cousins to play with. I want you to have that. But I want you to know I will always love you. You will always have a place in my heart." With those words, the baby squeezed my finger, and fell asleep. I must have dozed off too because I was startled awake by a knock at the door. I looked down at the baby, who was still sound asleep on my chest. "Come in."

I assumed it was the Swansons, but to my surprise, it was Mrs. Goodwin. I gulped in shock and almost dropped the baby.

"Mrs. Goodwin, what are you doing here?"

She wiped a tear from her eye. "Your mother told me you had the baby. She's Sam's, isn't she?"

I nodded. "Yes. But I'm not keeping her. Her adoptive family is on their way."

As if on cue, the baby started to cry.

"You should have told me I was going to have a grandchild," Mrs. Goodwin said. "I could have helped. You didn't have to go through this alone."

The baby started to cry louder, and Mrs. Goodwin reached out her arms. "May I hold her?"

I slowly handed the baby to Mrs. Goodwin, who gently rocked her back and forth. She seemed to have the magic touch because the baby stopped crying right away. Mrs. Goodwin, on the other hand, started bawling like a baby.

"She looks so much like Sam did when he was a baby."

I nodded. "She has his eyes. And his hair."

Mrs. Goodwin looked at me, with pleading eyes. "I want you to reconsider giving her up for adoption."

I shook my head. "I can't do that. I promised the Swansons I wouldn't do that."

"I'm sure they are really nice people," Mrs. Goodwin said as she rocked the baby back and forth. "But they didn't know Sam. They can't tell her stories about her daddy to keep him alive in her heart. She's the only thing left that is a part of my son. I want to see her grow up. I need to see her take her first steps and say her first words. And I know it won't be easy, but I want you to know I am here to support you every step of the way. There is a job waiting for you at Goodwin Financial when you are ready to work, and the guesthouse can be yours, rent-free, for as long as you need it. Now, I know we didn't exactly start things out on the right foot, but I want the chance to make that up to you. Once the adoption is final, there is no turning back. You still have time, Rachel, so I am begging you to change your mind."

I just sat there in silence because I had absolutely no idea what to say. The thought of breaking the Swansons' hearts again was unbearable, but I felt a huge wave of guilt that I didn't tell the Goodwins they were having a grandchild. Finally, my words came out slowly.

"I'm sorry I didn't tell you. I guess I was just overwhelmed and scared. Nothing has felt right since Sam's been gone. I haven't felt like myself for a really long time."

Mrs. Goodwin put one hand on my shoulder while she cradled the baby with the other. "I understand. None of us have been ourselves without Sam, but this little one can heal us. He can live on through her. In the end, this is your choice. I can't force you to keep her, but I want you to know you have all the support you need to give her a good life."

With those words, she kissed the baby on the top of the head and placed her back in my arms. Then she reached into her purse and pulled out an envelope, which she placed on my bedside table before she stood up and walked out of the room. I sat there holding the now sleeping baby until my curiosity got the best of me and I reached for the envelope. Inside was a check, and the amount was enough to change everything.

CHAPTER

34

When I heard another knock at the door, my heart started drumming faster in my chest. This was the moment I had wanted to avoid since Mrs. Goodwin had left, but I knew there was no turning back. As I looked into the eyes of my daughter, I knew what I had to do. Giving her up would be like giving up my own heart. I would have to break their hearts. But how?

"I heard our girl made an early appearance!" Amy chirped as she and Dan walked into the room and straight over to get a look at the baby. I held her a little closer to my chest.

"Yeah, I guess she likes to get a head start on things."

Amy reached out her arms. "Thanks so much for taking care of her until we could get here, but we've got this now. Can I hold her?"

I pulled the baby even closer to my chest, and Amy's smile turned into a look of concern.

"Is everything all right with the baby?"

I nodded. "Yes, of course. She's perfect. It's just ... We need to talk."

Amy and Dan Both looked like I had punched them in the stomachs, and I had to look away. I couldn't watch them go through the pain I was about to cause.

"Don't tell me you changed your mind," Dan said, and when I didn't answer, they knew. They both fell to their knees, sobbing.

Of course, I started bawling, but I managed to force my words out through my tears. "I'm so sorry. I didn't think I would be able to take care of her or give her what she needs, but Mrs. Goodwin came, and I know that I can. I lied to you. Sam's parents never knew about the baby. I guess I was just stubborn and immature, and I probably don't even deserve to be her mother, but I know I have to try. If I don't, I will regret it the rest of my life." My voice trailed off, and my throat tightened up.

Dan stood up, the pain on his face replaced with anger. "How could you do this to us? We shared our story with you. We trusted you! You promised you wouldn't do this!" Amy stood up, sobbing into his chest, and he wrapped his arms around her. I felt like the most horrible person on the planet, and I wanted to make it right. I wanted to take the hurt away. All of a sudden, I heard the sound of a baby crying, and it came to me.

"I'm sorry that I can't give you this baby," I said quietly. "But there was a baby born in the room next door that needs a good home, and I know that baby is meant to be yours."

Just a little while later, Mom, Grandma, and Michelle were back with a bag of extra clothes and toiletries. They even remembered my favorite vanilla-scented lotion, which I was grateful for because my skin had never been so dry. I wasn't sure if that was normal after childbirth, but I couldn't wait to lather it all over my body.

"I thought the Swansons would be here by now," Mom said, looking puzzled.

"They were," I answered.

"But you still have the baby?"

I looked down at the sleeping baby, who had just finished a bottle. I was still trying to decide if I wanted to breastfeed, but I was overwhelmed. Less than an hour ago I was ready to hand her to the Swansons, and now she was mine. That was terrifying and exciting all at the same time.

"Yeah, about that. I'm keeping her." They all looked at each other, stunned.

Michelle couldn't hide her excitement. "Does that mean I really get to be her auntie?"

"Yes, it does. Would you like to hold your niece?"

"Of course I would!"

Michelle reached out her arms, and I handed her the baby, who grunted as Michelle rocked her back and forth.

"I'm going to be the best aunt ever. I promise."

"I know you will, kiddo," I said. "And I'm going to need all the help I can get too."

"I still don't understand," Mom said. "What about the Swansons? They must be absolutely heartbroken."

"They were, but I think everything is going to work out for them. They are talking to Jessica right now, and I'm pretty sure they're going to adopt her baby. I know this wasn't the plan, but when I held her, I fell in love. I just can't imagine my life without her. And Mrs. Goodwin had something to do with it too. She stopped by, you know."

Mom put on her best fake surprise face. "Really?"

"Yes, really. And she told me that you told her, so don't even pretend to be surprised."

She let out a huge breath. "I'm sorry if I overstepped boundaries, sweetie. I know you didn't want me to tell them, but I just felt like they had a right to know they were having a grandchild. I mean, I would want to know if I were them. I would want to at least have the chance to say goodbye before the baby is with her new family."

"Well, instead she told me all the reasons I shouldn't give her up, and she made a lot of sense too. Nobody else is going to keep Sam alive for her. We can tell her stories, show her pictures, and make sure she knows who he was. She also offered me a job and a place to stay, so I know I will be able to take care of the baby."

"So, you aren't too mad at me?" Mom asked.

I looked at Michelle, who was beaming as she stroked the baby's head. "No, I'm glad you told her. If you didn't, we would be having a completely different conversation right now."

Mom stood in front of Michelle and held out her arms. "Okay then. It's my turn. Can I hold this little bundle of joy?"

Michelle looked disappointed, but she handed the baby over to Mom, and she and Grandma both looked down at the baby with happy tears in their eyes as they coed and talked to her in a silly high-pitched voice that everyone seems to do with babies. I had already promised myself I was going to talk to her in my normal voice, but the baby did seem to look up like she was listening to every word.

"She's so beautiful," Mom said. "Absolutely perfect."

"I agree," Grandma chimed in. "But I just have one question. Now that you've decided to keep the baby, what are you going to name her?"

I smiled. I had given some thought to that question since the Swansons left, and there was only one name that really fit her.

"Samantha," I said. "I'm going to call her Sam."

CHAPTER

35

I always knew there was something different about Samantha. When she was a baby, she always seemed to be looking (and sometimes smiling) at something or someone only she could see. When she was a toddler, she started talking to these imaginary people she insisted were real. Everyone said she just had an active imagination and she would grow out of it, but I knew better.

As she got older, these tendencies only got stronger. She would become very upset if she couldn't help her special friends with their unfinished business. She said it was her job to help them. These were the times I really missed Sam. He would be able to guide her in a way I never could.

When her first-grade teacher called me in for a conference to discuss Samantha's concerning behavior, I knew exactly what we would be talking about. This teacher never seemed to like Samantha and had mentioned how she was always daydreaming instead of focusing on her schoolwork. I knew she was smart; as a matter of fact, she was at the top of her class. Her daydreaming didn't affect her schoolwork; it just annoyed the teacher. But I walked in with an open mind, ready to defend my daughter if I needed to.

"Hello, Mrs. Tate. Sorry I'm late. I got held up a bit at work."

She pushed a strand of her jet-black hair behind her ear. "Miss Walters, I'm glad you could come. Have a seat."

I sat in the chair across from her and suddenly felt like I was back in third grade. "So, you wanted to talk to me about Samantha?"

"Yes. I've been very concerned. She seems to be fixated on these imaginary people. The other day, she never came in from recess. Another staff member found her out on the playground, talking to herself. And yesterday, she drew this."

She pulled out a picture that looked like a person who seemed to be holding his chest with red crayon smeared all over, most likely to represent blood. There was a thought bubble over the person's head that said, "Help me."

I took a deep breath and shrugged. "She has an active imagination."

Mrs. Tate just shook her head. "She's been talking to herself during class too. I really think Samantha should be evaluated by the school psychologist. These behaviors just aren't normal."

All of a sudden, the mother bear came out in me. I wanted to leap across the desk and strangle Miss Tate, but I managed to keep my cool.

"With all due respect, who are you to say what's normal and not normal? Samantha is a very smart little girl, and I wouldn't change a thing about her. She almost always gets 100 percent on every test, so maybe the problem is you. Maybe she just needs a more challenging environment."

THE PROMISE

Mrs. Tate seemed taken aback. "I just want to help Samantha."

"Well, maybe she doesn't need help. Did you ever stop to think that maybe she's not talking to herself? Maybe someone is there, but you just can't see them. Just because you can't see something doesn't make it less real."

Mrs. Tate didn't seem to have an answer for that.

Just then, Samantha came bursting into the classroom, her blonde pigtails bouncing up and down. She looked more and more like her daddy every day. "Mom, can we go home now?"

"Yes, sweetie. I think Mrs. Tate and I were just finishing up."

Samantha noticed the picture on Mrs. Tate's desk and went to pick it up. "Mrs. Tate?"

"Yes, Samantha?"

"Is this what you wanted to talk to my mom about?"

Mrs. Tate nodded. "That is one of the issues I wanted to talk to her about."

Samantha studied the picture and pointed to the person who was holding his chest. "That's your uncle Steve, Mrs. Tate. And he says he knows who shot him."

I swear Mrs. Tate turned as white as a ghost. "What did you just say?"

Samantha sighed. "He knows who shot him. He says it was William. He wants him to go to jail so he can't hurt anyone else. He says William is dangerous."

Mrs. Tate took a while before she was able to answer. "But how could you possibly know that? I've never talked about my uncle Steve."

Samantha just shrugged. "I just know."

I felt like a deflated balloon at that point. I had no idea how to help my daughter navigate in a world in which people sometimes didn't understand her.

"Come on, Samantha. It's time to go." I grabbed her by the hand and pulled her out of the classroom, leaving Mrs. Tate speechless.

"Why are you in such a hurry?" Samantha demanded as we walked out the door and toward the parking lot. "I wanted to tell her that her uncle Steve can't cross over until William is punished, and he's about to hurt someone else. We have to stop him."

I bent down to her level and looked right into her beautiful blue eyes. "Sammy, sweetie, I know you want to help, but you can't help everyone. Especially closed-minded people like Mrs. Tate. I think it is best is you keep these things to yourself."

Her face changed from one of confidence to one of defeat and confusion. "I don't understand. You tell me to be myself all the time, and when I do, you tell me not to."

"That's not what I meant," I said on the verge of tears. "What did you mean then? Do you wish I was normal? Because I want that all the time. I just want to be like everyone else!" With that, she stomped to the car, climbed into her booster seat, and buckled herself in.

I slid into the driver's seat and started the ignition. It broke my heart when I looked in the rearview mirror and saw my daughter's tear-streaked face.

"Sammy, you know I love you more than anything, right?"

She nodded and wiped a tear from her eye.

"You are the best thing that has ever happened to me, and I love you just the way you are. I don't want you to change just to please someone. I want you to be yourself because Samantha Grace is awesome. So, don't be afraid of what other people think, okay? I will always have your back."

"Thanks, Mommy. I love you too."

Even though my words seemed to calm her, we still drove home in silence, which wasn't like Samantha at all.

∽∞∽

"Hey, kiddo, how was your day?" Michelle greeted Samantha as we walked in the door. She had offered to babysit so I could have a girls' night out with a couple of friends, which was something I really needed right about now. Even though she had a busy life working at a local preschool and working toward her degree in social work, she always made time for her niece.

"Okay, I guess," Samantha answered as she set her backpack down.

"That doesn't sound too enthusiastic," Michelle said. "I I have an awesome night planned that will turn that frown upside down. First, we can paint our nails, and then we can watch *Frozen* while eating your favorite pistachio ice cream."

Samantha rolled her eyes. "I don't like that movie anymore. If I have to hear that song again, I'm going to scream!"

Michelle looked confused. Up until a few weeks ago, that was Samantha's favorite movie. "Okay, we can watch something else then."

"Okay. Thanks, Auntie Michelle. I'm going to my room for a while," Samantha said with a sigh as she walked into her room and closed the door behind her.

"Rough day?" Michelle questioned, gesturing toward the closed door.

"You could say that. I had a meeting with Sammy's teacher."

"How did that go?"

"Not so great. Mrs. Tate has never been a big fan of Sammy anyway. She was very concerned about her imaginary friends. She even suggested we see the school psychologist."

Michelle shrugged. "Well, I love her imagination. Maybe Mrs. Tate is the one who needs a psychologist."

I sighed. "I know we all love to say it's her imagination, but the fact is, it's very real. These people Samantha talks to, they aren't pretend."

"What?" Michelle looked confused. "I don't understand." I realized I had never shared Sam's abilities with anyone.

That was a promise I had made to him, and one that I had kept. But he had been gone almost seven years. I had faced the fact that he was never coming back. And keeping this secret was eating me alive. I wanted to share it with someone. And If anyone would believe this crazy story, my sister would. So, I just spat it out, right then and there.

"Sam could communicate with dead people, and so can Sammy."

"Really? I mean, I always knew he was different, but wow." Michelle and I both sat down on the couch, lost in our thoughts for a while.

"When did you know? Did Sam tell you?"

I nodded. "He talked to our dad, you know. He told me things he never could have known unless he had talked to him. He even knew the words to that song he used to sing to Mom."

Michelle looked around, in disbelief. "Do you men to tell me Dad is still walking around, watching us?"

I shook my head. "No. He crossed over a long time ago, before Sam disappeared. I was there when it happened."

Michelle's jaw dropped. "And you never told me any of this?"

"I'm sorry," I said, meaning it. "I promised Sam I wouldn't, and I always keep my promises. He never wanted people treating him different, and I don't want that for Sammy either. But I'm afraid that's impossible now."

"How come?"

"Because she told her teacher today that she knows who murdered her uncle. She even drew a picture of it. I thought Mrs. Tate was going to faint."

Michelle let out a huge breath. "What did Mrs. Tate say? Did she still think Sammy is just making it up?"

"I couldn't tell. I drug Sammy out to the car and told her to keep these things to herself, but that only made things worse. She said she wished she was normal, like everyone else."

Michelle put her hand to her heart. "Poor Sammy. I hate that she feels that way. She's such an awesome kid."

I nodded. "Yes, she is. I just wish I knew how to help her. The only person who would really understand where she's coming from is Sam. I would give anything for just one more day with him, you know?"

Michelle wrapped her arms around me. "He's still with us, even if you can't see him. I know he is."

My sister's words did give me some comfort, but somehow, it just wasn't enough.

CHAPTER

36

I met Jessica and Brianna at a new nightclub called Long Shots. It had been a long week, so it was great to spend time with old friends. Girls' night out was supposed to get my mind off of things, but I couldn't stop thinking about Samantha. I guess that was one of the side effects of parenthood. It really was a 24/7 job.

"How's Sammy doing?" Jessica asked.

"She's doing fine," I answered. "Still as spunky as ever. How about Miranda? She just had a birthday, right?"

It wasn't hard to remember since it was the same day as Samantha's.

"Yes, it was awesome. The Swansons invited me. I love the fact that I can have a small part in her life. She had a jump house and a pinata and a ton of gifts too. She's getting so big, and she loves her little brothers."

Jessica held out her phone and pulled up a picture of an adorable strawberry-blonde girl along with two little boys. When Miranda was just a baby, The Swansons found out they were pregnant all on their own with identical twin boys they named Parker and Mason. It's funny how life works itself out sometimes.

"We're not supposed to be talking about kids," Brianna reminded us. "It's girls' night out, remember?"

"So, what are we supposed to be doing then?" I asked. "We're all a little rusty at this."

"Well, I don't know about you two, but I am on a man hunt tonight," Brianna answered, taking a sip of her beer. "It has been way too long, if you know what I mean."

Brianna had always had bad luck in the love department. I, on the other hand, didn't really try. I had never really dated anyone since Sam. Part of me felt like I would be betraying his memory if I moved on. And I was always so busy with work and Samantha, there really wasn't much time. Besides, would it be fair to date anyone if I would always be comparing him to my one true love?

Just then, the bartender placed three fresh beers in front of us. "These are from the gentlemen over on the corner," he told us, gesturing toward a group of three men sitting together, smiling and waving sheepishly.

"I'm going for the blonde one," Jessica said, winking at one of the men, who winked back.

Before I knew it, Both Jessica and Brianna were deep in conversation with two of the men, laughing like they were the most fascinating people on earth. Reluctantly, I finally walked over to the solo man, who seemed shier than the other two. He was good-looking, with light brown hair, green eyes, and a broad chest that looked like he must work out.

"Hi, I'm Rachel," I said, introducing myself.

"I'm Mark. Nice to meet you."

"Looks like our friends are getting along," I said, gesturing toward Jessica and Brianna, who were chatting it up with the other two men.

"Looks like it," he agreed.

"Thanks for the drinks." I held up my beer and took a sip of it.

"You're welcome. We weren't sure what you liked, so we just told the bartender to send whatever you were drinking."

"Well, it's really good. We're not picky. We're just happy to be out on the town with no responsibilities. We try to have a girls' night out once a month, but with kids and other responsibilities, it doesn't always happen."

"I know how that is," he said, taking a long pull of his beer. "So, you have a kid?"

I nodded. "Yes, a girl. She's six."

Mark looked relieved. "I have a five-year-old son. Most people don't want to date someone who has kids, so I haven't dated much since my divorce. My friends actually forced me to come out with them tonight."

I finally let out a breath I didn't realize I was holding. "I totally understand."

The rest of the night fell into a relaxed rhythm as we shared stories about parenting, work, and life in general. Mark was a middle school English teacher, and I could tell he really loved what he did. I could tell by the way his face lit up when he talked about his students. I told him about my job at Goodwin Financial, which I was very grateful to have, but I was a little jealous of the passion he had for his job. For me, work was just a paycheck. I guess I never really thought about what I was passionate about. My main goal was providing for my daughter. Of course, I wouldn't give her up for anything. Sammy was the one great thing I'd done with my life so far. Mark felt the same way about his son, whom he shared custody of with his ex. He must have gone on for an hour with stories about Ryan, who seemed to have the same spunky nature as Samantha. By the end of the night, I felt something I hadn't felt for a long time. I could see my life with someone besides Sam, and that was exciting and terrifying at the same time.

CHAPTER

37

Monday mornings were always rough, and the following Monday was no exception. My alarm failed to go off, so when I finally woke up and saw what time it was, I jumped out of bed and sprinted for Samantha's room. She was curled up in a ball under her pink comforter, and she groaned when I told her it was time to wake up.

"Come on, Sammy. If we don't hurry up, you'll be late for school, and I'll be late for work. I need your help this morning. Get dressed, brush your teeth, and meet me in the kitchen, okay?"

"Okay," she mumbled as she slowly crawled out of bed. After I had brushed my hair and teeth and splashed some water on my face, I came out to the kitchen where Samantha was waiting for me. She was staring blankly at a local news station on the television.

"Mommy, look!" she said, pointing to the screen.

"We don't have time this morning," I said. "Besides, I don't like you watching the news. It's too depressing."

"But they arrested William!"

I watched as the anchorwoman looked into the camera with a solemn expression on her face.

"A local man has been arrested in connection with several murders, including his own brother, Steve Tate. William Tate was a well-liked part of the community, a professor at a local college, and a father to three daughters. After a tip from an anonymous source, police searched his home where they found pictures of the deceased victims, as well as the murder weapon. No further information is known at this time, but we will follow this story tonight on the five o'clock news."

I grabbed the remote and turned the television off. "Sammy, was that Mrs. Tate's Uncle?"

She nodded. "Now Steve can cross over. Isn't that great?"

∞

When I dropped Samantha off at school, she ran up to Mrs. Tate, looking more excited than I had seen her for a while.

"Mrs. Tate, they arrested William!"

Mrs. Tate bent down to her level, her expression was softer now. "I know. And that never would have happened if you hadn't told me what you knew. I owe you an apology, Samantha. I should have had more of an open mind. You really do have a gift."

Samantha shrugged. "I was just trying to help. At least he can't hurt anyone else, right?"

"That's right," Mrs. Tate said with a smile. "And from what the police found, he was already planning on hurting more people. Thanks to you, he won't have the chance. He's going to be in jail for a long time."

"Good," Samantha answered. "I'm sorry it was too late for your uncle Steve. He was a great guy, and he wanted me to give you a message."

Mrs. Tate raised her eyebrows, curious. "What's that?"

"Never give up, no matter what," Sammy answered, and she walked off to put her back pack away.

"That sounds like Uncle Steve," Mrs. Tate whispered before she turned to me. "I owe you an apology too. Your daughter is one amazing little girl. They found a detailed list of William's past and future victims. It makes me sick to think I went to family gatherings with him. It just goes to show you never truly know someone. Anyway, I do hope you accept my apology."

"Of course, I do. I know better than anyone that it's a lot to take in." I looked at Samantha, who was sitting in her desk with her pencil in her hand and a huge smile on her face that reminded me of Sam's. Everything about her lately seemed to remind me of Sam. "And, Mrs. Tate, I would appreciate if you would keep Sammy's abilities on the down-low. I really just want her to be treated like any other kid."

She smiled. "Of course I will. Now, if you don't mind, I have a class to teach."

Mrs. Tate headed to the front of the class, and they all started with the Pledge of Allegiance. I remembered starting class the same way when I was her age, and I thought to myself that some things never change.

When I slipped into my desk as Goodwin Financial, I found at least a hundred emails waiting for me to answer them. It was going to be a very long day. I started to get to work when Norma Goodwin came in, waving a paper in the air.

"This customer is on my last nerve! He wrote another nasty email this morning. Rachel, would you be a darling and call him back for me? Politely tell him we can't have him as a client if he treats our staff this way. I would do it, but you're so much better with difficult clients than I am."

"Sure, I'll get to that after I answer all of these." I gestured toward my computer screen.

"Thanks. You're the best. I don't know what we'd do without you."

Somehow, instead of a compliment, her words were like a punch in the gut. I continued typing away. When I finally looked up, I noticed Norma sitting across from me with a concerned look on her face.

"Is everything all right, Rachel? You don't seem like yourself this morning."

"Everything's fine. I've just been busy."

"And Sammy? How is my granddaughter? I feel like I've been at work so much I've hardly seen her."

"She's doing fine."

"Is she still talking to those imaginary friends?"

I shrugged. "I guess so."

"You know, Sam used to talk to people to. But I always knew they weren't imaginary."

I stopped typing and looked at Norma, wondering what she was getting at. Then she answered my question for me.

"I knew about Sam's abilities—that he could talk to dead people. I always knew."

My eyes widened. "You did?"

"Of course I did. His father was the one who wanted him to see a child psychologist to have him deprogramed. I loved

Sam for who he was." She wiped a tear from her eye before she continued. "I just wish I'd had the chance to tell him that."

I reached over and squeezed her hand. "I'm sure he knows."

"But we'll never really know for sure, will we?" Norma didn't wait for an answer before she continued. "I would give anything just one more day with Sam."

"Me too," I agreed, letting the memories with Sam wash over me like a wave on a warm summer day.

"But what I want more than anything is closure," Norma said quietly. "I want to know what happened to my son, and if someone is responsible, I want them to pay. Is that too much to ask?"

I shook my head. "No. I want that too, but I don't think it's ever going to happen."

"But what if … You're going to think I'm crazy, but what if Samantha could help?"

"How could she help?" I asked.

Norma took a deep breath. "She does have Sam's special abilities, doesn't she?"

"Yes, she does. I would have told you sooner, but I honestly didn't think you'd believe me."

She waved a hand in the air. "Don't worry about that. I know what it's like to raise such a special child, and it isn't always easy, is it?"

"No, it's not," I said, relieved to finally find someone who understood.

"Anyway," Norma continued. "If Sammy can communicate with others who have passed on, why not Sam?"

I sat in silence for a minute, letting that sink in. I don't know why it never occurred to me that Sammy might communicate with Sam. Of course, I'd always kept him alive through stories and pictures, but she'd never said anything about talking to him. I didn't want to get my hopes up. I'd already accepted the fact we might not ever have answers about what happened to Sam.

"I'm not sure if that's possible," I said, looking down at my computer screen and then back up at Norma.

"Why not?" Norma questioned with a desperate look on her face.

"Because Sam might have already crossed over. From what he told me, once the deceased cross over, that's it. They can't communicate with the living anymore. Besides, I don't want to stress Sammy out trying to make her do something that isn't possible."

Norma nodded. "She's one lucky little girl to have you for her mother, you know? You always put her first. And Sam was lucky to have you in his life too. I'm really sorry for all of those times I tried to come between you two. I guess I was just scared of Sam making the wrong choice, but you were always the one for him. I never told you this, but one day when he came home after spending the day with you, he said 'Mom, I think I'm going to marry this girl.' I laughed at the time, but I know he meant it. He was in love. I'm so glad that in his short life, at least he had that."

I smiled, knowing that I felt the same way about Sam, and part of me always would.

"I want to thank you for something too, Norma. I want to thank you for coming to the hospital that day and encouraging me to keep Sammy. I can't imagine my life without her."

"You don't need to thank me for that," she answered. "I just helped you figure out what you already knew."

"Yes, you did," I agreed. "And why were on the subject, there's something I've been wanting to talk to you about."

"What's that, dear?"

"Well, I'm very grateful for all you have done for me and Sammy, but I'm feeling like it might be time for a change."

"What kind of change? Are you unhappy with your pay here at Goodwin Financial? Because I can talk to human resources and get you a well-deserved raise."

"It's not that. My salary is more than enough. I just think it might be time for me to figure out what my dream is, if that makes any sense."

A knowing smile spread over her face. "It makes perfect sense. I just want you to be happy. After all, you're like the daughter I never had. I want you to know the guesthouse is yours for as long as you like, and this job is here as long as you need it. And if you ever need a letter of recommendation, just let me know."

"Thanks," I said.

"No problem. Now I guess we should get back to work. This place isn't going to run itself, is it?"

"No. It definitely won't," I agreed as I tuned back to my computer and started typing.

CHAPTER

38

The rest of that week was probably about the slowest and most boring week ever, but it led up to Friday night, when I had a dinner date planned with Mark. We had talked a few times during the week, and the conversation seemed to flow easily. Something about him made me feel relaxed and content, like I could talk to him about anything. Of course, I was still nervous about going on a real date for the first time in seven years. I was just a little bit out of practice. And Samantha didn't like the idea of me going on a date at all. She had tried to think of any excuse to get me not to go, but I knew it was because she was used to having me all to herself.

"Can you please hold still?" Michelle said as she tried to help me with my mascara.

"It feels like you're going to poke me in the eye," I told her.

"That's only because you keep moving!"

We both laughed, and she dabbed a little bit of mascara on the tip of my nose.

"Don't be nervous," she assured me. "You've got this."

"I know I do. It just feels weird, you know?"

"I know, but you need to get yourself out there. In twelve short years, Sammy will be going off to college. It seems crazy, but that time will come before you know it. Do you really want to be alone the rest of your life?"

I shook my head. "No, I don't."

"Then you have to do something about it," she said as she continued working on my makeup.

"Are you sure this isn't a little much?" I asked, looking myself over in the mirror.

She shook her head. "Trust me. You look marvelous, darling."

Just then, the doorbell rang, and Samantha ran to the door and flung it open. My mom stood there with a big smile on her face.

"How's my favorite granddaughter?" she asked, scooping Sammy up in her arms. "Are you ready for our girls' night out?"

Sammy giggled. "I've been ready all day!"

Grandma and Norma Goodwin came in behind her, looking like they were ready for a night on the town. They had all planned a night out with dinner and a movie while I went on my date. I was happy to have any type of distraction for Samantha, especially since she wasn't a huge fan of me dating.

Grandma looked like she was having one of her good days. Lately, she had been having a hard time getting around, and just recently, we'd had to take away her car keys. It was hard for her to give up that independence, but so far, she seemed to be taking it well. She'd even adopted a cat, whom she named Pickles. When I asked her why on earth she would name a cat Pickles, she said simply, "I like pickles."

"How are my favorite girls?" Grandma asked, coming to give me and Michelle a hug.

"We're doing great," I said. "Thank you, guys, for making such a fun night for Sammy. I know she's been looking forward to it."

"No problem at all," Mom answered. "We've all been wanting some time with our favorite girl. Take your time, and have a nice night."

"Yes, take your time," Norma agreed. "We don't all get together like this often."

"Well thanks again," I said. "Just don't keep her up too late. She does have a soccer game in the morning."

"Oh, we would never do that," my mom said sarcastically as she winked at Sammy.

Sammy winked back with a sneaky grin on her face. The doorbell rang again, and this time, I knew it must be Mark. All of a sudden, my heart started pounding, and I had butterflies in my stomach. I held my breath as I walked to the door and opened it. Mark stood there, wearing a black polo shirt and some jeans.

"Hi, Rachel. Sorry I'm a little late. Traffic was a nightmare."

"That's okay. Come on in." I gestured toward the living room, where my mother, grandmother, Norma, Michelle, and Sammy all stood, staring at him like they were inspecting him. I thought to myself that it must have felt just a little intimidating to walk in to that many people, especially on a first date.

"I didn't know I was joining a party," Mark said nervously.

"You're not," I assured him. "This is my mom, my grandmother, and my sister, Michelle. And this is my daughter, Sammy, and her other grandmother, Norma. They all came over to watch Sammy and have a girl's night out together."

"That sounds like fun," Mark said, turning his attention to Sammy. "Hello, Sammy. I've heard a lot about you."

Sammy rolled her eyes, and I could tell already this conversation wasn't going to go well.

"Hi, Mark. I've heard a lot about you too. I just want to tell you a few things about my mom before you go on your date."

Mark smiled. "Sure, anything that might help me to know her better."

Sammy cocked her head, deep in thought. "Well, first of all, do not let her eat beans. They give her really bad gas. Second, she has a really bad habit of picking her boogers and eating them. And third …"

I began to feel the heat rise in my face. This kid was going to be the death of me. "Samantha, can I see you in your room for a minute?"

I didn't wait for her to answer before I took her by the hand and led her into her room. I closed the door behind us and knelt down to her level.

"Sammy, why were you trying to embarrass me in front of Mark?"

"I don't like him," she said with a shrug.

"You don't know him, and he just happens to be a really nice guy."

"Well, he's still not good enough for you."

"Let me be the judge of that. Okay? I have just a little more life experience than you do. I think I can take care of myself. And just because I go on a date doesn't mean I won't have time for you, if that's what your worried about."

"It's not that," she said in an almost whisper.

"What is it then?"

"Well, it's just ... What if Daddy comes back?" She picked up the picture of Sam she kept on her nightstand and traced her finger over it.

I sighed, trying to find the right words. "Sweetie, he's not coming back."

"How do you know?"

"Because I just do. The police searched for him for a long time. If he was coming back, don't you think someone would have found him by now? I want to believe he could come back as much as you do, baby. But that just isn't going to happen."

"But he's alive! I know he is!" Samantha seemed to believe what she was saying with every fiber of her being.

"Where is he then? If you're so sure your dad is out there, where is he?"

Samantha looked down at her feet. "I don't know, but I know he's alive."

I thought about what Norma had said, and I looked my daughter in the eyes. My heart was pounding at the thought that she might have some sort of answer about Sam's whereabouts. "How do you know that? Have you talked to him? I want you to tell me the truth."

She shook her head. "No, I haven't talked to him, and that's exactly how I know he's alive. My daddy would never cross over to the other side without saying goodbye to me first!"

I was at a loss for words because part of me knew she might be right. But the logical side of me took over.

"Your dad is gone, Samantha, and you and I both need to accept he's not coming back. Okay?"

She set the picture of Sam back on the nightstand and wiped a tear from her eye. "Okay, Mommy. I won't talk about it anymore. Go ahead and go on your date, and I'm sorry for what

I said to Mark. You can tell him those things I said about you aren't true. Well, except that beans do give you gas sometimes."

We both giggled, and I wrapped my arms around her and held her for a while, taking in the scent of her strawberry-scented shampoo. I thought to myself that she probably wouldn't want me to hold her like that much longer, and I was going to cherish every minute of it as long as I could.

CHAPTER

39

I tried to relax and enjoy my date with Mark, but my mind seemed to be somewhere else. I kept replaying my conversation with Sammy in my mind, trying to make sense of it all. Then I reminded myself that although she was wise beyond her years, she was still only a six-year-old child, and six-year-olds didn't always make sense.

"I hope you like Asian food because we can always go somewhere else if you aren't a big fan," Mark said, looking through his menu.

"No. I love Asian food. I'm sorry if I seem distant. It's just been a really long week."

Mark smiled. "I know exactly how you feel. Life can be exhausting, especially when kids are involved. Between work, Cub Scouts, and soccer practice, I feel like I'm always on the move."

I breathed a sigh of relief, glad to be with someone who understood how challenging parenthood could be. "I want to apologize for Samantha. I think she just has a hard time letting go."

"I totally understand," Mark assured me. "Ryan isn't a big fan of me dating either. He even tried to pretend to be sick so I would stay home with him, but I knew he was faking it."

I laughed. "Kids will try to say anything to manipulate us, right?"

"That's right," he agreed. "It's like we're just their humble servants, here to meet their every need."

The waitress stopped by to refill our waters and take our order. We had already decided on the blues dinner, which had a variety of seafood. Apparently, we both had a love for anything with shrimp. We sipped on our wine while we waited for dinner. A relaxed sort of silence filled the air for a while; neither of us needed to say anything.

Finally, Mark broke the silence. "It was really nice meeting your family tonight."

"Thanks," I said. "I hope it wasn't too overwhelming for a first date. I know they can be a lot."

"Not at all. They seemed like a great group of people. So, Norma is Sammy's grandmother? Is Sammy's father involved in her life at all?"

I gulped, not prepared to talk about Sam. But somehow, I knew the conversation might come up.

"Well, not exactly. It's kind of a long story, but the short version is he went missing before Sammy was born, actually on the day I found out I was pregnant. You might have heard of the Sam Goodwin case? It was all over the news for a long time."

His face flashed with recognition. "I do remember seeing that. At first, they thought it might be a ransom case because he came from a wealthy family, but there was never a note or anything, so then they thought foul play might be involved. But they never found a body, right?"

"That's right. They did find his car but no body."

He shook his head, sadly. "That must be really hard—to never have closure. I mean, at least if they had found a body, you could have laid him to rest. It must feel like you're in limbo."

"Sometimes," I agreed. "But I've just had to pick up the pieces and move on. I honestly don't know if I could have done it without Sammy. She's the only thing that keeps me grounded sometimes."

Mark nodded in agreement. "I'm sorry if I brought up painful memories for you. I know that must not be easy to talk about."

"It's all right," I assured him. "How else are we going to get to know each other, right? But I do feel like you know more about me than I do about you."

"Fair enough. Ask me anything."

"Okay. Well, how about your ex?" I asked. "How is your relationship with her?"

Mark cleared his throat before he answered. "We try to get along, for Ryan's sake. I think we are better as friends and coparents than we ever were as a married couple. It turns out we just wanted different things in life, but we will always have Ryan in common, and we both want what's best for him. We share custody, so I have him one week, and she has him the next. It seems to work for now, but as Ryan gets older and schedules change, we're both flexible. We understand that things might come up, and we might have to switch days sometimes. And we always go to his school events together."

I thought about what it would have been like to raise Sammy with a partner and how much she was missing not having a strong male role model in her life. I was just a little older than her when my dad died, but he was still such a big part of who I was. I was grateful for all of the help I got from my mom and sister and the Goodwins, but my heart still ached for her sometimes.

"I think it's great that you're able to put your differences aside for your son's sake," I told him. "I would love to meet Ryan sometime. Maybe we could get the kids together for a play date?"

Mark beamed. "I would love that."

For the rest of the night, the conversation flowed freely, and I finally felt like I was able to be in the moment and enjoy myself. And even if things didn't work out with Mark romantically, I knew I had found a friend for life.

CHAPTER

40

Goodwin Financial was abuzz with activity on Monday morning, and I never thought I would catch up on all of the emails and phone calls. And just when I thought I was catching up, Mr. Goodwin stomped in and placed a stack of papers on my desk.

"These are all of the new clients that need to be filed right away," he said. "Did you ever hear back from Mr. McAlister?"

I shook my head. "Nope. I think he decided to go with someone else."

He sighed. "I was really hoping to get that account. Could you at least try to call him back please?"

"Sure."

"Thanks, Rachel. I hope you realize how much we appreciate you around here. Norma told me you were thinking about leaving Goodwin Financial. Is that true?"

I shrugged. "As much as I appreciate everything you guys have done for me and Sammy, I just feel like it might be time for a change. But don't worry. I don't have anything in the works quite yet, and I wouldn't leave without giving you plenty of notice first."

"That's good to know," he said, relieved. "Let me know if I can help in any way, okay?"

"I will," I assured him. "Thank you."

Although Mr. Goodwin had a rough exterior, I knew without a doubt that he wanted the best for me and Sammy, and I was glad to have him as part of my support system. I continued answering emails and making phone calls until Norma came into my office with a panicked expression on her face.

"Rachel, there's a call for you on line 2."

"Who is it?" I asked, thinking that it might be Sammy's school.

"It's your mom," she told me. "Something about your grandmother."

My heart drummed in my chest as I sped to the hospital. I felt like I was on autopilot as I found a spot in the parking garage and ran into the waiting room, where my mother, Michelle, and Sammy were waiting for me.

"I hope you don't mind that I got Sammy out of school a little early," my mom told me. "I just felt like she deserved the chance to say goodbye too."

I ran over and threw my arms around my mother. "That's okay, but are they really sure she's gone?"

"I'm afraid so, Rachel. I went to her apartment this morning to check on her. I found her on the floor, and she barely had a pulse. The paramedics got there as soon as they could, but it was too late. She's on life support now, but she's technically brain-dead. They said it was a stroke, and it must have happened sometime in the middle of the night. I just talked to her last night before she went to bed, and she was fine." My mother's words were cut off by her tears, and we both held each other and cried.

Then I felt Sammy's little arms wrap around me. "Mommy, is GG dead?" She had always called my grandmother GG, which was short for great-grandma.

"Yes, sweetie. The doctors have her hooked up to machines to keep her body alive, but her spirit, the part that makes her GG, is gone."

"I want to see her."

"Okay, but you have to realize she isn't going to wake up. Okay?"

Sammy rolled her eyes. "I know that, Mom. I just want to see her one last time."

⁌⦵⦵⦿

Grandma's hospital room seemed so cold and sterile, and the machines that were breathing for her beeped in a steady rhythm. I held Sammy's hand as we walked toward her hospital bed, and I took Grandma's hand in mine and knelt down beside her.

"Hi, Grandma. I just want to thank you for everything. You have been there with me through some really rough times, and I really don't know what I would have done without you. You've been my biggest support, and I am who I am now because of you. I love you."

I kissed her hand as tears trailed down my cheek. Then I turned to Sammy, who was wiping tears out of her own eyes.

"Would you like to say something to GG, Sammy?" She nodded as she came up and laid her head on

Grandma's chest. "It's okay to go now, GG. I love you."

After Sammy said those words, Grandma's heartbeat slowed down until finally, all of the lines on her machine went flat. Sammy looked up at me with tears in her eyes.

"I'm going to miss her."

My own tears began to fall faster, and I wrapped my arms around my daughter. "I know, baby. Me too."

Suddenly, there was a gust of warm air, and Sammy looked up toward the ceiling and smiled. "Okay, GG. I will tell them. I love you."

She waved toward the ceiling, and then everything turned cold again, and I knew she was gone. Sammy looked me right in the eyes and smiled.

"Do you want to know what she said?"

I nodded. "More than anything."

"She said not to be afraid because there is a place more beautiful than you can imagine, and we'll all be together again someday. So, this isn't really goodbye. It's just see you later, alligator!"

I laughed, knowing that was something my grandma would have said and feeling a sense of peace that I hadn't for a long time.

CHAPTER

41

When someone you love passes away, sometimes it takes a while to sink in. I found myself calling Grandma when I wanted advice on a new recipe or when I just wanted someone to talk to. When her voicemail answered, it was like losing her all over again. And just when I thought I had it all together, something would remind me of her, and I would start crying again. Of course, I took some comfort in what Sammy had said, but somehow, it wasn't enough.

There was a lot to take care of the following week. Besides notifying all of her friends and family, we had to go through all of her things and decide who got what and what we would take to Goodwill. It's amazing how much stuff she had crammed in a tiny one-bedroom apartment. Luckily, for the big things, she had a will. We met with her attorney, who read it to us. Her voice was steady and even, and it was almost like Grandma was reading it herself.

"To my daughter Anna, I leave my car. You have to hold the key in the ignition a certain way, but I know you will figure it out. I also want Anna to have my designer jewelry collection and her father's Rolex watch. To my granddaughter Rachel, I leave my collection of romance novels and also my artwork because I know you will be the only one who will appreciate them."

Michelle giggled. "She's right about that."

"I also want Rachel to have my computer," the attorney continued. "It may be old, but It still works. And to my other granddaughter Michelle, I want to pay off your student loans. You know how much I hate debt. There is an account set up that will help you with that."

At the sound of her words, Michelle started to cry happy tears. She had been stressed over how she was ever going to pay off her student loans, and now she didn't have to worry about that anymore.

"As for the rest of my accounts, I want them to be split between my daughter, my two granddaughters, and my great-granddaughter. I would like Samantha's portion to go straight into a college fund for her.

"And finally, to my great-granddaughter Samantha, I leave my most prized possession of all, my cat, Pickles. Take good care of him."

Sammy jumped up and cheered. "I finally get to have a cat!"

I smiled, glad to see she was so happy. And although I wasn't looking forward to cleaning litter boxes and paying vet bills, it would be good for Sammy to help care for a pet.

We hosted a celebration of life at the Goodwins' house, and I was amazed at the number of people who came out to celebrate Grandma. Norma had it catered by Grandma's favorite Mexican restaurant, and we all had a chance to share stories about Grandma and how she touched our lives.

Mom stood up first and took a deep breath before she spoke. "When I think about my mother, I think about so many things. But most of all, I think about the way she was always there for me, no matter how difficult I made it. And believe me, I wasn't always easy. I was a very defiant and headstrong kid. I snuck out when I wasn't supposed to, and I talked back. I talked back a lot. But my mother never tried to crush my feisty spirit. She just calmly explained what my punishment was and that I needed to use a respectful tone of voice next time. I think the fact that she was so calm is what scared me the most. I expected her to yell and scream, but not my mom. It just wasn't in her nature.

"When my husband died almost seventeen years ago, my mom moved in to help take care of my daughters, no questions asked. That's when she watched me spiral into a whirlwind of drugs and depression until she couldn't take it anymore. I lost touch with my mother for almost ten years, and that is time I would give anything to get back now. But when I called her to tell her I was ready to get help and that I knew I couldn't do it without her, she was on a flight the next day. That is a loyalty you only get from a mother, and she was the best."

She turned her attention to me and Michelle before she continued. "I just wish I could say that I learned from her and that I was the mother my girls deserved, but I know I'm not. I've made mistakes—big mistakes that tore my family apart. I was so fixated on what I lost that almost forgot what I still have, which is a lot. I have my two daughters and my beautiful granddaughter. I have a job I love, and I've been clean for more than seven years."

With those words, everyone cheered. Michelle, Samantha, and I all ran to her and joined in a group hug.

"I'm so proud of you, Mom," I told her.

"Me too," Michelle said.

She just squeezed us tight. "I love you girls."

"We love you too, Mom."

Sammy looked up at us with a confused expression on her face. "Grandma, didn't you like to take showers?"

"Of course, sweetie. Why?"

"Because you said you've only been clean for seven years."

We all laughed, and I tussled her hair. "That's a different kind of clean, Sammy. We'll talk about that later. Okay?"

She shrugged. "Okay. Can I be the next to talk about GG? I have a few things I want to say."

"Sure," I told her. "I don't see why not."

Sammy climbed up on a step stool, and everyone turned their attention to her.

"I want to say that I know my GG would be so happy to see you all here today, and I know she loved you all. I didn't know her as long as most of you since I am only six, but she was my best friend. We used to play hide-and-seek together, and she would read to me whenever I went to her apartment. She read me fairy tales that she read when she was a little girl, and sometimes she would just make up stories. She was a great storyteller. Whenever I was sad, she would tell me a story that would cheer me up. And she liked to sing too. We used to sing together all the time, and she especially liked The Beatles. They were her favorite. So, in honor of GG, I would like all of you to sing along with me."

Sammy walked over to her karaoke machine, which was a gift from Grandma for her last birthday.

"Do you know what she's doing?" Mom asked.

I smiled. "I have no idea."

And with that, my daughter pushed a button and led us all in a beautiful rendition of "Ob-La-Di, Ob-La-Da."

And I thought to myself that I couldn't have said it any better.

∞

Later that night as I tucked Sammy into bed, I thought about what a perfect day it had been, and I could just imagine Grandma smiling down at us. I felt relieved that everything went as planned, and it was a wonderful tribute to an awesome person.

"I was really proud of you today," I told her as I pulled the covers up and kissed her on the forehead. "I know this has been hard on you too."

"I'm going to miss GG, but I know I'll see her again someday, so I guess that makes it a little easier," she said.

"Yes, it does," I agreed.

Just then, Pickles the cat climbed up on her bed and started rubbing his head against Sammy's.

"Mommy, do you think Pickles likes his new home?" she asked, stroking his fur.

He began to purr, which answered her question.

"I think he seems pretty happy," I told her.

"Do you think he misses GG?"

"I bet he does, but he's glad to have you as his new owner."

Sammy smiled proudly as she nuzzled the cat under her chin and listened to him purr.

"I love it when he purrs. It's so relaxing," she whispered.

I smiled, happy to see the bond between the two.

"I was thinking we could really use something to look forward to this weekend, and the fair will be in town. So, what do you think, Sammy? Would you like to go?"

She looked deep in thought for a minute. "Do you think I'm tall enough for the big Ferris wheel this year?"

"You've had a big growth spurt, so you just might be." She snuggled under her blanket and yawned. I knew she would be asleep in a matter of minutes. "Then yes," she said. "I want to go."

"Good. Now get some sleep."

"Good night, Mommy."

"Good night."

CHAPTER

42

Going to the fair had become our yearly tradition, and Sammy looked forward to it every year. Michelle usually went with us, but she had finals for one of her classes, so it was just the two of us. I didn't mind because it gave us a chance to have some much-needed mother-daughter time. The smell of funnel cakes filled the air, and music played in the background. A clown rolled past us on a unicycle, juggling some bowling pins. Samantha looked up at him with wonder in her eyes.

"Mommy, can I have a unicycle for my birthday?"

I smiled, knowing that she would change her mind at least ten times before her birthday came.

"We'll see, Sammy. You know, it's not as easy as it looks. That clown probably had to practice for a long time before he could ride like that. Now, what would you like to do first?"

"I want to see the horses," she said without hesitation.

"Okay. The stables are this way."

We went toward the back of the fair where the stables were and the big arena where they brought out the horses to run around. Samantha headed for a big black horse that was standing outside the stable while a teenage girl in a 4-H uniform brushed him.

"Can I pet your horse?" Sammy asked eagerly. She loved horses and had always dreamed of owning one, but because we still lived in the Goodwins' guesthouse, it just wasn't possible.

"Sure you can," the girl said with a smile.

Samantha stroked the horse gently with a big smile on her face. "What's his name?"

"This is Comet," the girl answered. "He's about eight years old."

"Wow, he's even older than I am," Sammy said.

I snapped a quick picture of Sammy with Comet. Then I thanked the girl for letting Sammy pet the horse, and we walked around the stables, looking at all of the horses. I lifted Sammy so she could say hello to each one, and they all seemed eager to have company. Finally, we made it to the end of the stables.

"Well, it looks like that's all of the horses," I told her. "It's hot outside, so why don't we head to one of the buildings so we can cool off for a while, and then we can go on some rides."

"Okay," Sammy said, taking my hand. As we started to walk away, she noticed all of the trailers and RVs parked in the back behind the stables. "Hey, Mommy, who stays in those trailers?"

"Oh, probably the people who are working the fair. Some of them don't live here in Sacramento, so they need a place to stay while the fair is in town."

"Don't they miss their homes?" she asked in disbelief.

I shrugged. "Maybe, but I'm sure they're happy to have a job."

She seemed to accept that answer, and we headed toward the building where the youth art exhibits were. I always admired the talent of the youth, some who weren't much older than Sammy.

"Do you think if I practice, I could make paintings like that?" Sammy asked, pointing to an oil painting of the ocean.

"I bet you could," I told her. "Would you like me to look into an after-school art class? I think there is one starting next trimester."

She nodded eagerly. "I would love that!"

We turned the corner, where I saw a familiar face. It was Benny promoting his youth art class. And standing beside him was Harry. They both seemed to recognize me right away and waved for us to come over.

"Hi, Rachel, long time no see," Benny said.

"Yeah, it's been a while," I agreed. "This is my daughter, Sammy. Sammy, this is Benny and his brother, Harry."

Sammy waved hello and scooted a little closer to me. She always had been shy around new people. I looked up at Harry and beamed. "I'm so glad to see the two of you together again."

"Well, it wouldn't have happened without your help," Harry said. "I've been wanting to thank you for whatever you said to my brother because after that, he started coming to see me in prison. He even went back to school to finish his law degree so he could get me out. So, here I am."

"Well, you look really good," I complimented.

"I feel really good, and I feel like I've been given a second chance—a second chance I never thought I would get. So, thank you again. Mostly, thank you for forgiving me at a time I couldn't even forgive myself."

I smiled. "You're welcome."

Harry scanned the crowd around us. "Are you still with that Sam guy? Because I'd like to thank him too. I know he played a big part in you coming out to see me that day." I shook my head. "Sam went missing over seven years ago."

Harry couldn't hide his disappointment. "I'm sorry to hear that. I guess I'm a little out of the loop."

"It's all right," I assured him. "If Sam were here, I think he would be just as happy as I am to see you guys together again."

"Do you think so?"

"I know so. Now, if you don't mind, I promised this little lady I would take her on some rides."

Benny smiled at Sammy. "You two have fun. And if you're ever interested, I have art classes for all ages." He handed a flyer to Sammy, and her eyes lit up.

"Mommy, we were just talking about doing an art class!"

"Yes, we were. I'll make sure to look into that." I looked at Benny and back at Harry, and I realized just how far I had come. There was a time I would never have felt this much peace around the man who, although unintentionally, ended my father's life.

"It was really nice seeing both of you," I said before Samantha and I walked away.

As we walked through the next building, the vendors tried to get us to try all of their products. Sammy was antsy to go on some rides, so I rushed past them, glad to have an excuse not to stop. I was ready to move on with my day too. Then, suddenly, Sammy stopped in her tracks. She was listening in on a conversation between Magic Mike, the self-proclaimed psychic medium, and a couple who appeared to be in their midthirties.

"I can see your son, and I know he is at peace," Magic Mike told the couple. "He wants you to know he's all right." Sammy tugged on my pant leg. "Mommy, why is that man lying to that nice couple?"

I shrugged. "I don't know, sweetie. Let's go on some rides, okay?"

She shook her head and crossed her arms over her chest. "No."

"But you've been looking forward to rides all day. What's the matter, Sammy?"

"That man told that nice couple he could see their son, but he can't! He's lying to them!"

"How do you know he's lying?"

"Because their son, Michael, is standing right beside me!" she shouted. "He had something called leukemia, and he died. He has a message for his parents, but that man can't hear him! Why would he lie to those nice people, Mommy?"

I sighed, remembering Sam's reaction to the very same psychic medium more than seven years ago, the last time I saw him in person. That night played in my mind like a wonderful dream I never wanted to end. Holding his hand as we walked through the fair, kissing him on the Ferris wheel under the stars. But I was brought back to reality when Sammy asked the same question, and I knew she wasn't going to let this go.

"Why would he lie like that?"

"I don't know, Sammy. Can we please just leave this building and go on some rides?"

She shook her head and marched over to Magic Mike on a mission.

"Excuse me, sir. Why are you lying to these nice people?" Magic Mike turned to her and laughed. "You're a cute kid, sweetheart. Do you want a sucker?"

"No, I don't want a sucker. I just want you to stop lying," she said. "It's not fair."

"Life's not fair, kid. I have bills to pay, so go find your mommy and leave me alone. Okay?"

"You are one piece of work, but you're no psychic medium!" Sammy spat out before she turned toward the couple.

I had that feeling of déjà vu when I remembered Sam saying the same exact words to him many years ago.

"Michael says thank you for making his last months here so fun," Sammy said to the couple. "He especially loved Disneyland. And he's really sorry he couldn't make it to his cousin Jackson's party, but he made a card for him. He says it's under his bed."

The woman seemed to be in shock as she looked at Sammy. "Did you know Michael, sweetie?"

Sammy shook her head. "I just met him about five minutes ago."

"But that's not possible."

Sammy gently put her hands on the woman's cheeks. "Anything's possible when you believe."

The couple both looked at her in awe.

"Is there anything else Michael wanted us to know?" The man asked.

Sammy took a step back. "There is something, but I'm not supposed to tell."

The couple looked disappointed, and the man put his arm around the woman to comfort her.

"Oh, I guess I'll tell you anyway," Sammy said. "You're going to have another baby."

The woman's eyes widened, and she turned toward the man. "I am a little late," she whispered. "I just assumed it was because of stress."

"Michael doesn't want you to be afraid to love this new baby," Sammy continued. "He says he knows how much you loved him, and he wants you to love this baby just as much." Just then, Magic Mike stood up between Sammy and the couple. "What are you trying to do to me, kid?"

All of a sudden, I felt the urgent need to get Sammy out of there, fast.

"Samantha, let's go!" I said sternly, reaching out to take her hand. For a brief second, I made eye contact with Magic Mike, and his eyes flashed with recognition.

"Hey, I remember you."

I ignored him as I pleaded for Sammy to come with me, but her feet were planted firmly on the ground. She wasn't going anywhere without a fight. Magic Mike bent down and whispered something in her ear before I was able to pick her up and walk away with her.

"Your kid is just like that guy you were with, you know," Magic Mike called. "What was his name again?"

I turned around to face him, feeling all of the heat rise in my face. "His name was Sam."

The couple he was talking to were collecting their things to leave.

"You can't leave until you pay," Magic Mike demanded. "If we're going to pay anyone, it's that little girl right there. You're just a phony trying to steal money from grieving people!" the man said as they walked away.

I followed after them as magic Mike called out. "You just cost me a customer! You're going to pay for this! Do you hear me?!"

But I just kept walking until Sammy and I were safely outside. I breathed a sigh of relief when I didn't see Magic Mike anywhere in sight.

"Are you all right, Sammy?" I asked.

"Of course I'm all right. I'm just mad at that mean man. He shouldn't lie to people."

I bent down to her level and looked her in the eyes. "Well, not all people in the world are nice. Some are greedy, and they just think about themselves. I want to ask you something, though. I saw him whisper something in your ear. What did he tell you?"

She shrugged. "Nothing important."

I narrowed my eyes, giving her my best mean mom look. "You know how important it is to always be honest with me, right?"

"Yes."

"Okay. Well, I can see you're really upset, so do you want to leave the fair early today? It will be in town for two weeks, so we can always come back."

"No. I want to stay until it's dark out!" she insisted. "You promised we would go on the Ferris wheel."

Part of me was disappointed that she wanted to stay because I was emotionally exhausted. But I knew how much she was looking forward to the Ferris wheel, and I hated to disappoint her.

"Okay. The rides are this way."

After a couple of rides, we played a dart game. Samantha won a stuffed bunny, which she was excited about because she had never won anything by herself before.

"I think I'll name him Billy the bunny," she said proudly. "Isn't he cute?"

"He's very cute," I agreed. "But it's hot, so how about some shaved ice?"

She beamed. "That sounds yummy."

On the way to the shaved ice stand, we ran into the nice couple who were talking to Magic Mike earlier, and they stopped to thank Sammy for what she had told them about their son.

"It's been hard since we lost Michael," the woman said. "But your daughter helped us to find peace, so we'd really like to thank her in any way we can. We were going to pay that Magic Mike guy for his services, so we can pay her instead." She reached into her purse for some money, but Samantha shook her head.

"I don't want money. I just want to help people."

The couple looked at each other, shocked at Sammy's reaction. "Are you sure?"

She nodded. "Michael seemed like a nice kid. I'm glad I got to meet him before he crossed over. And don't worry. You'll see him again."

"Well, thank you again," the man said. "It means a lot that you came to talk to us when you could have just walked away. And you were very brave standing up to Magic Mike the way you did."

"Thanks, but I was mostly mad," Sammy said. "I hope that man loses his job so he can't take people's money and lie to them."

"So do we," they agreed.

"Oh, and there's one more thing Michael told me to do, but I ran out of time."

"What was that?"

Sammy ran up and gave them each a hug. "That's from Michael."

The look on both of their faces was priceless, and I knew that although it wasn't easy raising a child like Samantha, moments like these made it all worth it. We said goodbye to the couple and headed for the shaved ice stand, where I ordered each of us a cherry-flavored shaved ice. I fumbled for some cash in my wallet and counted out exact change. I remembered from my days at Burger Shack how much easier that made things. Then I paid the vendor and turned around with two shaved ices in my hand.

"Here you go, Sammy. Sammy?"

I scanned the area where she had been standing just seconds ago, but she was nowhere to be seen. "Sammy, where did you go? This is not funny, you know. This isn't the place for hide-and-seek. Sammy, if you can hear me, come out now!" When there was no answer, my heart sank deep in my chest. "Sammy?! Sammy!"

But there was still no answer, and that's when panic set in.

CHAPTER

43

I called out Sammy's name until my voice was hoarse and my throat was sore. I pulled up the picture on my phone that I had taken of her next to Comet the horse that day and showed it to anyone who would listen. I said the same thing over and over again.

"Have you seen this little girl? Her name is Samantha. She goes by Sammy. She's six years old, about four feet tall, and she was wearing a pink T-shirt and a pair of denim shorts."

But everyone who saw the picture just shook their heads and walked away. Suddenly, the world began to spin. I threw the shaved ice in the trash because it was hard to balance while holding my phone, and I really didn't feel like eating it anymore. Finally, I found a security guard, a tall and lanky man with dark hair. I held up my phone with the picture of her. By then, I was out of breath, and every word took more effort.

"Excuse me, sir. My daughter is missing. This picture was taken today. Her name is Sammy. She's six years old." He nodded. "I'll put the word out to the other security guards. Kids wander away all the time, and most of the time it turns out fine. Did you check the lost and found? If anyone found her, that's where they'd take her."

"Thank you." I sprinted over to the lost and found, but she wasn't there. They took my cell phone number and promised to call if she showed up. So, I continued to run around like a chicken with my head cut off, calling Sammy's name with no answer and no sign of her in sight.

Finally, I collapsed from exhaustion on a bench, crying into my hands. Where could she be? It wasn't like Sammy to wander off like this. One minute, she was standing right beside me, and the next, she was gone. I thought about all of her favorite places at the fair and where she might have gone, and suddenly I had an idea.

First, I headed for the Ferris wheel. She had talked nonstop about going on the Ferris wheel, so maybe she was near that area. I ran through the line, showing everyone her picture and asking if they had seen her, but nobody had. After walking the entire line with no sign of her, I felt like a deflated balloon. Then I looked at the picture I had taken of her earlier by the horse, and I knew I couldn't give up yet. I still had another idea.

I raced back to the stables where the girl in the 4-H uniform sat outside the stable, reading a book.

"Excuse me," I said. "My daughter came to pet your horse earlier, and now she's missing. I was wondering if you'd seen her?" I showed her the picture on my phone, and she nodded almost immediately.

"Yes, I saw her just about ten minutes ago. She came through here and asked to pet Comet again. I thought it was kind of strange that she was by herself, but she told me you were meeting her here in a few minutes. Then she went that way."

She pointed toward the trailers and motor homes behind the stables. I remembered Sammy asking me about them earlier, but I didn't think anything of it. Now I just wondered why on earth she would come all the way back here.

I thanked the girl and headed to the area where all of the trailers were, and almost immediately, I spotted her little pink rabbit lying on the ground. She loved that toy, and I know she wouldn't just leave it there willingly, so I knew something was very wrong. My stomach was in knots as I picked up the little pink bunny and held it tightly to my chest.

"Sammy, baby, where are you?" I whispered.

And it was that moment that I heard the most beautiful sound of my daughter's voice.

"Mommy, Mommy!"

Before I had a chance to say anything, she ran to me and jumped in my arms. I was relieved and angry at the same time.

"Sammy, what on earth are you doing over here? I was worried sick! You know better than to wander away from me like that!"

"I know, and I'm sorry, but I have something to tell you."

"Well, you can tell me at home because we are leaving right now. No Ferris wheel for you, young lady. You almost gave me a heart attack."

"I don't care about the stupid Ferris wheel anymore, but we can't go home, Mommy."

"Why not?"

"Because I found him."

"Found who?"

"I found Daddy, but I can't wake him up. I think he needs help. Come on! I'll show you where he is."

Before I even had time to process what she was saying, Sammy pulled me toward a tan motor home with green stripes. There was a star on the door that said "Magic Mike."

"He's in here. Hurry!"

"Sammy, wait," I cautioned. "This is Magic Mike's motor home."

"So?"

"So, we can't just go into someone's motor home. It's called trespassing. And how do you even know it's your dad?" She rolled her eyes. "There are pictures of him all over our house. It's him. What do you call it when someone takes another person away from their family?"

"Kidnapping."

"Exactly, so come on!"

Sammy pushed on the door with all of her might before it finally opened and pulled me into the motor home, which smelled of garbage and old food. Fast-food wrappers littered the floor, but she rushed me past the kitchen area to a back room where there was a bed. Someone was lying in the bed, and my heart jumped out of my chest. As I came closer, I realized it was an older, thinner version of Sam with more facial hair than I remembered. It was definitely him, and as I looked down at his arm, I realized something very disturbing. He was handcuffed to the bed.

"Sam?" I said in disbelief, trying to wake him up. "Sam, can you hear me?"

But there was no answer, and when I looked down at my daughter, she was crying.

"Is he going to be okay, Mommy?"

"I don't know, baby."

Her tears started falling faster. "I'm so sorry I lied to you. When you asked what Magic Mike whispered in my ear, I said nothing. But he told me he knew where my daddy was. I didn't want to get your hopes up until I knew he was telling the truth. I remembered how you said some people who work at the fair live in these trailers, so I came here and found the one with his name on it. Then I found Daddy lying here, but I couldn't wake him up. I hope you aren't too mad at me."

I wrapped my arms around her. All of a sudden, everything was starting to make sense. I didn't know why I hadn't thought of it before. Magic Mike was behind everything.

"I'm not mad at you, sweetie. I'm glad you brought me here. But we need to get all three of us out of here, fast, before Magic Mike comes back."

I frantically shook Sam, but there was no response. Then I pulled on the handcuffs that tethered him to bed, but they weren't going anywhere. I looked for a key or at least something small I could trip the lock with, but there was nothing.

"Sam, wake up!" I said frantically. And finally, his eyes started to flutter open.

"Rachel?" he said in a weak voice. I rushed to his side. "Yes, it's me."

"What are you doing here?"

"Someone told me I might find you here," I said, stroking his hair.

He looked over at Sammy, squinting his eyes to focus. "Who's this?"

Sammy came up to him, placing her hands on each side of his face. It was the most heartwarming thing I had ever seen.

"Hi, Daddy. I've been waiting my whole life to meet you."

Sam's expression changed to one of shock.

"Daddy? I have a daughter?"

I nodded. "We have a daughter. It's a long story, but I'll fill you in later. Right now, we need to get you out of here. Do you know where the key to the handcuffs might be?"

Sam cleared his throat and struggled to force out his words in a weak voice. "Mike keeps it on a key ring on his belt loop, but you have to promise me you won't go near him. He's dangerous, Rachel. You need to leave right now."

I knelt down beside him and placed my hand on his. "I can't leave you now. I just found you."

We all jumped when we heard a voice behind us say, "Well, well … What a nice little family reunion."

I looked up to see Magic Mike standing there with a smirk on his face, and he was holding a gun.

CHAPTER

44

For the first time, Sam's voice was loud and clear. "You leave them alone, Mike. They have nothing to do with this!"

Mike just laughed in an eerie sort of way. "Well, maybe your girlfriend doesn't, but the kid sure does. Do you know she just cost me a customer, the same way you did the day we met? Like father, like daughter."

Sam's eyes widened, and he seemed to understand exactly what he meant. "I'm sorry I'm not living up to your expectations lately, but did you ever think it's the drugs you keep me doped up on? Maybe if you stopped giving me those, I could do what you want again."

Mike shook his head. "There's a problem with that because it's the only thing that keeps you from running away. I think it's time I got some fresh help with my business, so I seem authentic again. And the kid already showed me she's got the gift."

I felt my anger come to a complete boil, and the mother bear came out in me. I lunged toward Mike and tried to grab the gun from him. We struggled for a while until he dropped the gun, and a shot went off.

"No, Mommy!" Sammy screamed with tears trailing down her face.

I froze in shock until I realized the bullet had pierced a hole in the wall. We both dove for the gun, which was lying on the floor, but Mike was quicker and stronger. Just like that, he was in control again, holding the gun to my head.

"Don't try anything like that again, lady, or you'll be sorry!"

"Just leave them alone!" Sam demanded.

"It's too late for that," Mike said. "The kid is going to be my link to the other side. The only question is, what do I do with the two of you because you know way too much."

Suddenly, a light bulb seemed to go off in his eyes. He grabbed his cell phone out of his pocket and quickly dialed a number. "Yes, Officer. I have an emergency situation. A couple just broke into my motor home and tried to rob me! They had a gun, and I just shot both of them in self-defense. I'm in parking spot number 3, behind the stables. Hurry, come quick!"

He slipped his phone back into his pocket, looking proud of himself. My heart was drumming in my chest, and my mind was racing, trying to think of a way to get the three of us out of there, quick. I stood in front of Sammy, instinctively trying to shield her from any danger.

"You will take her over my dead body," I said to Mike, but he just laughed.

"That can be arranged." He reached for something on his belt loop, and seemed enraged when he couldn't find it. "Where did my key go? It won't make me look good if he's handcuffed to the bed."

Before he could say another word, Sam jumped up from the bed with the key in his hand, which he used to stab Mike right in the eye. Mike screamed in agony, holding his eye as blood squirted all over the floor.

"What the hell, kid?" He fell to the floor and dropped the gun.

Sam jumped down and grabbed it, and suddenly, we were in control again.

"I could shoot you dead right now, but I want to watch you suffer for what you've done to me," Sam said, holding the gun to Mike's temple.

For the first time, Magic Mike looked scared. As a matter of fact, he looked terrified. And that's when two police officers pushed open the door and stormed in, holding out their guns.

"Freeze, and put your weapon down!" they shouted in unison.

Mike slinked down, making himself look like the victim. "They both tried to rob me, Officers! I tried to fight them off, but they overpowered me, and that young man threatened to kill me!"

Sam rolled his eyes. "Give it up, Mike. You're going down."

"Drop your weapon!" the officer demanded again.

Sam sighed and placed the gun on the floor. "He's not the victim here, Officers. He kidnapped me seven years ago, and he's been keeping me as his prisoner ever since."

Both of the officers looked puzzled, still holding their guns toward Sam.

"It's true," I said. "Have either of you heard of the Sam Goodwin case? He disappeared seven years ago."

They both shook their heads. "Sorry, lady, I have no idea who you're talking about."

"Don't you ever watch the news?" I asked in disbelief.

The taller one shrugged. "Not really."

I rolled my eyes. "Seriously? And you're supposed to be our law enforcement? Well, I feel really protected right about now."

"They're telling the truth!" Sammy shouted. "I found my daddy, and he was handcuffed to the bed!"

The officers looked at each other, not letting go of their guns.

"Hey, Marvin, I think I do remember that case about the Sam Goodwin kid." The shorter one said. "His dad was the head of Goodwin Financial, remember? They never figured out what happened to that kid. Do you think that could be him?"

The officer pulled out his phone and flipped through some articles until he found one about Sam. He looked at the picture of the boy in the article and then at the man who stood before him. But while he was looking down, Mike dove for the gun that was lying on the floor and jumped up, pointing it straight at the officers.

"These are just a couple of angry clients. They broke into my motor home and tried to rob me!" he shouted.

The officers raised their guns. "Drop your weapon!"

Mike tried to make a run for it, but the officers overpowered him and knocked him off his feet. And it was the most satisfying feeling in the world when they slapped a pair of handcuffs on his wrists.

"Mike Vernon, you are under arrest for kidnapping and assaulting an officer!"

I held Sammy in my arms, and Sam put his arm around me. We all let out a sigh of relief, knowing that it was over.

"You have the right to remain silent. Anything you say or do can be used against you in a court of law. You have the right to an attorney. If you can't afford one, one will be appointed to you. Do you understand these rights as they have been told to you?"

CHAPTER

45

Just a short while later, I sat in the hospital waiting room. I was waiting for an update on Sam. They had taken him back for a checkup, and his nurse, Roselyn, who happened to be the same nurse who took care of him after the Burger Shack explosion, promised to give me an update as soon as she knew anything. I had already called his parents and my mom to let them know he was alive and well. Of course, they didn't believe me at first. I'm not so sure I would believe such a crazy story if I hadn't just gone through it myself.

Sammy sat at a children's table in the corner, coloring a picture for Sam. She was exhausted but seemed to be doing well considering the trauma she had just been through.

"Do you think he will like this?" she asked, holding up a family picture that included herself, me, and Sam. Of course, she'd included Pickles the cat, who sat proudly in the corner with his tail in the air.

"I think he'll love it," I told her as nurse Roselyn came dancing into the waiting room.

"Looks like our miracle boy is at it again. He's going to make a full recovery. He might need some occupational and physical therapy to help him get stronger, and he might have some effects from all of the sedatives he was given, but other than that, he looks great."

"That's good to hear," I said with a smile. "This still doesn't feel real. I mean, I can't believe he's alive."

"Well, if you want some time with him alone, I would do it now," the nurse told me. "I'm sure his parents will be here soon, and as soon as the news reporters get hold of this story, you can bet this hospital will be a three-ring circus. I can watch your little one for a minute if you want."

As I sat in Sam's hospital room across from him, it seemed almost like no time had passed at all. Of course, there was a lot to fill him in on. So much had happened in the last seven years, but one thing remained the same. There was a connection between us that was hard to describe. He told me about how Mike had run him off of the side of the road on the night he took him and knocked him out with some sort of tranquilizer. The next thing he knew, he woke up tied down in his motor home, and Mike was demanding he contact people who had died to make him look more authentic. I told him about my life since he'd been gone, most of which was pretty unbelievable to someone who hadn't been around for the last seven years.

He shook his head in disbelief. "Let me get this straight. Jessica Sinclair is your best friend, and you work at Goodwin Financial and live in my parents' guesthouse?"

I nodded. "Yep. And don't forget we have a daughter."

"I guess a lot can happen in seven years," he said quietly.

"Yes, it can," I agreed.

"Well, Sammy is an amazing little girl. I can tell you've done a really good job with her," he complimented. "Did you know she snuck me the key to the handcuffs while Mike had his back turned?"

"That sounds like her," I said. "If it weren't for her, I'm not sure I would have found you."

"So, you've told her about me?" he asked.

I nodded. "I wanted her to know who her father was."

"And she's like me? I mean, she can talk to dead people?"

"Yes, she can. She's pretty amazing. She even told me you were alive. I wish I had listened to her more. And do you want to know the ironic part? I was going to give her up for adoption. I had a family picked out and everything. But on the day I had her, your mother came to the hospital to talk me out of it. She said she wanted to keep you alive somehow. That's when she offered me the job and the house."

"Wow. My mom really did that? Well, I guess it doesn't surprise me. She did always like to be in control."

"Actually, she left it up to me. She said in the end it was my decision, but she wanted the chance to watch Sammy grow up. As soon as I held her, I knew she was mine. I couldn't imagine my life without her."

"What about the couple who was going to adopt her? Weren't they upset?"

"They were at first, but they ended up adopting Jessica's baby, and now they have two boys. So, everything worked out."

"Well, I'm glad you kept her, and I'm sorry you had to go through all of that without me. I've missed so much of her life, but I want to make up for lost time."

I nodded. "We have all the time in the world now."

He smiled. "Yes we do."

I bent down to kiss him, but we were interrupted when Sammy came barreling into the room with nurse Roselyn following behind her.

"Sorry. I tried to hold her off as long as I could," the nurse said with a wink.

"Daddy, I made this for you!" Sammy said, holding up the picture she'd made.

"I love it," Sam said, holding out his arms, which Sammy gladly ran into.

"I'm so glad we found you, Daddy," Sammy said, burying her head in his chest.

"So am I," Sam agreed, wrapping his arms around his daughter with a look on his face that was pure peace.

And I knew at that moment that everything was going to be all right.

SIX MONTHS LATER

Our spot by the river still seemed to have its magical glow as we walked along the riverbank, this time with our daughter between us. It had been a long and emotional six months for sure. Sam needed some physical therapy to help him get strong again and talk therapy to help him emotionally. That wasn't surprising, as he had basically spent seven years of his life as a prisoner. He had a lot of pent-up anger about the time he had missed with his family, and understandably so. But he was getting better every day. His relationship with his parents was better than it had ever been, and as for us, we had decided we were going to take things slow for a while. Of course, that only lasted about a week. I guess you can't deny true love.

The bond between Sam and our daughter was incredible. It was like they had never been apart. They both seemed to have their own language and spent a lot of time helping people with unfinished business cross over. Sometimes I was a little jealous that they shared a bond over something I would never truly understand, but mostly I was happy Sammy had someone in her life who was just like her.

Sam had become quite a celebrity since he came back, and people stopped us all the time to ask if he was that Goodwin kid who went missing. He would always happily answer any questions they had, but there were some things he just didn't want to talk about. When the police questioned him after he came back, it came out that he was a medium. So now he works for the special crime unit, using his gift to help solve murders. He seems to take pride in his job, even though it can be emotionally draining at times. But he says it's all worth it when a bad guy is put in jail.

I was busy working on a book about our life, which was going to be available to the public soon. There was something about the computer my grandma had given me, and when I sat down to type, the words just started to flow. She always said she saw me as a published author, and it turns out she was right. I still work part time for Goodwin Financial, but now I'm part of the advertising department, which seems to suit me well.

"Hey, Daddy, do you think this is a good one?" Sammy asked, holding up a smooth, flat rock.

Sam examined the rock. "It looks like it. Why don't you give it a try?"

Sammy squatted down with a serious look on her face, like she was about to do the most important thing in the world. Then she threw the rock like a frisbee toward the water and squealed with delight as it skipped across the water, leaving a trail of ripples.

"I did it!" she said, running to give Sam a hug. He beamed with pride. He'd been trying to teach her to skip rocks all afternoon, and she finally did it.

Sammy skipped over to our tree and ran her fingers across our names. We had recently added her name to the tree, and she came to see it every time we went to the river.

"I love coming here," she said. "But there's just one problem with the tree."

"What's that?" Sam and I asked in unison.

"It needs another name."

"Another name?" I asked, confused.

"Like the name of my new baby brother or sister," Sammy said, matter-of-factly.

Sam and I looked at each other with our mouths open in surprise.

"Where did you hear you were having a brother or sister?" I questioned.

She shrugged. "Just a hunch."

I squeezed Sam's hand, and we both laughed. After all we had been through, we knew we could handle anything the future had in store for us, even if that included another child.

"Did you pick out a dress for the wedding?" Sam asked, trying his best to change the subject.

I nodded. "It's actually really pretty for a bridesmaid's dress."

Jessica had asked me to be a bridesmaid in her wedding. After Sam came back, I introduced her to Mark, and the two of them had been inseparable ever since. I was happy that two of my closest friends had found happiness with each other. Of course, I was still waiting for the day Sam popped the question, but I knew that would happen in its own time.

"Are we almost there?" Sammy asked as she skipped ahead of us.

"Almost where?" I asked.

Sam grinned and kissed my hand. "You'll see."

We followed Sammy as she led us to an open area by the riverbank. My heart skipped a beat when I saw what was spelled out in small rocks along the sandy shore.

Will you marry me?

I looked at Sam, who was grinning from ear to ear. Then he pulled something out of his pocket and knelt down on one knee.

"Rachel Walters, I have loved you since the moment I met you, and I can't imagine my life without you. We have been through so much together, and I know we can handle whatever life throws at us. So, will you marry me?" He held out a beautiful ring with a huge grin on his face. He knew my answer before the words left my lips.

I stared at the ring in awe before I was able to give him my answer. "Yes. Of course I'll marry you."

He slipped the ring on my finger, and we kissed while the river played a relaxing melody that only we could hear. Then I looked at Sammy, who stood there with a sneaky little grin on her face.

"Did you have anything to do with this?" I asked.

She nodded. "Daddy and I came here earlier today, and I helped him find the rocks to spell out the words. But I knew he was going to ask you for a while now. I helped pick out the ring too. Isn't it pretty?"

I nodded. "It's beautiful."

I scooped her up in my arms, and we all stood there, staring out at the river, in awe of its beauty. I was reminded of all the people who had passed on before us—my dad and grandma, just to name a few. Death was something I used to be afraid of, but not anymore. Because I knew now, beyond a shadow of a doubt, that I would see them again someday.

ABOUT THE AUTHOR

I've had a passion for writing since I was young, and I've always had a vivid imagination. I love a good story, and two of my favorite authors are Nicholas Sparks and Jodi Picoult. I am a sucker for a good romance, especially when I can relate to the characters. Although Sam and Rachel in the Promise are fictional, I hope you love them as much as I do.

This is my fourth novel, and I always try to write about controversial topics that people of this day and age can relate to. Domestic violence, drug addiction and mental illness just to name a few. If my stories help someone find hope through hard circumstances in life, it is well worth all the time and energy I put into writing them.

I live in Sacramento with my husband Jim and two children, Kyle and Kaitlyn who are growing up way to fast! I attended American River College where I studied early childhood education, and now I work with preschool age children. When I'm not writing, I love to spend my spare time traveling and seeing the world. I want to thank my family for being so patient through the long and sometimes tedious task of writing a novel. I love you all and hope you enjoy the promise. I promise it will not disappoint.